"AFTER 'EM!" FALCONI YELLED. "GO! GO!"

The Black Eagles detachment swept forward against the Viet Cong. The flapping bullets from both sides cut leaves and branches off trees with gardenerlike precision. It looked like an easy victory, but Falconi suddenly shouted, "Hold up! Cease fire! We're going back!"

"Ain't this a hell of a way to make a living," Paulo asked as they loped toward the rear through dripping vegetation.

"Knock off the noise!" Falconi snapped as they reached an area of fallen trees. The lieutenant colonel didn't waste time assigning fighting positions to each man.

Archie Dobbs glanced around. "Damn, sir! Looks like we're setting up an ambush."

"Give the man a cigar," Falconi said, pointing out a place for Gunnar's machine gun. "That's *exactly* what we're doing!"

#16
MONSOON HELL HOLE

THE BLACK EAGLES

JOHN LANSING

ZEBRA BOOKS
KENSINGTON PUBLISHING CORP.

ZEBRA BOOKS

are published by

Kensington Publishing Corp.
475 Park Avenue South
New York, NY 10016

First printing: August, 1988

Printed in the United States of America

This book is dedicated to
Biff and Lisa

Special acknowledgment to Patrick E. Andrews

THE BLACK EAGLES ROLL OF HONOR
(Assigned or Attached Personnel Killed in Action)

Sergeant Barker, Toby—U.S. Marine Corps
Sergeant Barthe, Eddie—U.S. Army
Sergeant Bernstein, Jacob—U.S. Marine Corps
First Lieutenant Blum, Marc—U.S. Air Force
Sergeant Boudreau, Marcel—U.S. Army
Chief Petty Officer Brewster, Leland—U.S. Navy
Specialist Four Burke, Tiny—U.S. Army
Sergeant Carter, Demond—U.S. Army
Master Sergeant Chun, Kim—South Korean
  Marines
Staff Sergeant Dayton, Marvin—U.S. Army
Sergeant Fotopoulus, Dean—U.S. Army
Sergeant First Class Galchaser, Jack—U.S. Army
Lieutenant Hawkins, Chris—U.S. Navy
Sergeant Hodges, Trent—U.S. Army
Mister Hosteins, Bruno—ex-French Foreign Legion
Petty Officer Second Class Jackson, Fred—
  U.S. Navy
Chief Petty Officer Jenkins, Claud—U.S. Navy
Petty Officer First Class Johnson, Sparks—
  U.S. Navy
Specialist Four Laird, Douglas—U.S. Army
Sergeant Limo, Raymond—U.S. Army
Petty Officer Third Class Littleton, Michael—
  U.S. Navy
Sergeant Makalue, Jessie—U.S. Army
Lieutenant Martin, Buzz—U.S. Navy
Petty Officer Second Class Martin, Durwood—
  U.S. Navy
Sergeant Matsamura, Frank—U.S. Army

Staff Sergeant Maywood, Dennis—U.S. Army
Sergeant First Class Miskoski, Jan—U.S. Army
Staff Sergeant Newcomb, Thomas—Australian Army
First Lieutenant Nguyen Van Dow—South Vietnamese Army
Staff Sergeant O'Quinn, Liam—U.S. Marine Corps
Sergeant First Class Ormond, Norman—U.S. Army
Staff Sergeant O'Rourke, Salty—U.S. Marine Corps
Sergeant Park, Chun Ri—South Korean Marines
Sergeant First Class Rivera, Manuel—U.S. Army
Petty Officer Third Class Robichaux, Richard—U.S. Navy
Sergeant Simpson, Dwayne—U.S. Army
Master Sergeant Snow, John—U.S. Army
Staff Sergeant Taylor, William—Australian Army
Lieutenant Thompson, William—U.S. Navy
Staff Sergeant Tripper, Charles—U.S. Army
Staff Sergeant Valverde, Enrique—U.S. Army
First Lieutenant Wakely, Richard—U.S. Army
Staff Sergeant Whitaker, George—Australian Army
Gunnery Sergeant White, Jackson—U.S. Marine Corps

ROSTER OF THE BLACK EAGLES

Lieutenant Colonel Robert Falconi
U.S. Army
Commanding Officer
(16th Black Eagle Mission)

First Lieutenant Ray Swift Elk
U.S. Army
Executive Officer
(14th Black Eagle Mission)

Sergeant Major Top Gordon
U.S. Army
Operations Sergeant
(14th Black Eagle Mission)

Sergeant First Class Calvin Culpepper
U.S. Army
Demolitions Supervisor
(14th Black Eagle Mission)

Sergeant First Class Malcomb McCorc
U.S. Army
Medical Corpsman
(14th Black Eagle Mission)

Staff Sergeant Paulo Garcia
U.S. Marine Corps
Intelligence/ Communications
(6th Black Eagle Mission)

Sergeant Gunnar Olson
U.S. Army
Logistics
(4th Black Eagle Mission)

Petty Officer 3rd Class Blue Richards
U.S. Navy
Demolitions Specialist
(9th Black Eagle Mission)

Corporal Archie Dobbs
U.S. Army
Detachment Scout
(14th Black Eagle Mission)

PROLOGUE

The young Viet Cong guerrilla sat comfortably in his perch in the high tree.

His position, secured by expertly tied planking, was roomy and made his task easier. He could plainly make out the entire layout of Camp Nui Dep that lay just beyond the tree line where he was concealed. The garrison's mortar positions, entrenchments, various dugouts and bunkers, and the landing strip were clearly visible to him. The VC worked diligently on his project, carefully sketching all these details. His natural talents were so great that the drawing was almost to scale.

After more than a week tending to this task, he was now in the final phases of it. The only thing left to do was to put in the ranges of the camp's various points for the benefit of the mortar crews. They would be servicing the Soviet M1937 82-millimeter mortars that would rain down a roaring hell of explosive and flying shards of steel on the camp.

The VC performed his task with high-powered

artillerist binoculars that had range indication scales imprinted on the viewing lenses. He picked out each potential target: a supply dump, various bunkers, points of strong defense, and other places where a spirited defense might slow down or stop any attackers.

A rumble of thunder in the sky behind him caught his attention. The Viet Cong broke his concentration long enough to look back at the sky. The black monsoon clouds were building up fast over southeast Asia.

He looked back at Camp Nui Dep. The inhabitants of the garrison would never expect an assault, much less the murderous one planned for them, during this season of wind and rains.

He smiled to himself as he put the finishing touches on his map.

CHAPTER 1

The incident would be forever recorded in the annals of the Black Eagle detachment as the Night of the Lutefisk.

Lieutenant Colonel Robert Falconi and his eight men had been transferred from the billets at Peterson Field in Saigon out to the wild hinterlands of the Vietnamese War. Their new home—where they had been stationed before on previous occasions—was a Special Forces "B" camp named Nui Dep. The reason for this banishment to the boondocks was Falconi's disregard of direct, lawful orders from Brigadier General James Taggart to abandon a mission and return from enemy territory.

The incident occurred when the Black Eagle detachment was neck-deep in North Vietnamese troops while conducting a raw, kick-'em-in-the-balls campaign of guerrilla warfare in the middle of the enemy's own territory. When the orders came to pull out it had a bad effect on the Black Eagle detachment. They had lost too many men in the past during equally dangerous situations. It almost seemed an insult to their memories and also to the integrity and guts of the survivors. Damning military tradition, Falconi put the situation to a vote: Pull out to certain safety and survival, or stay and slug it out with the very real potential of getting wiped out to the man.

The Black Eagles voted 100 percent to stay.

Thus, Falconi thumbed his nose at the general and went on to win that small part of the war.

It is an undisputed military fact that brigadier generals do not like lieutenant colonels to tell them to take their orders and cram them where the sun don't shine.

When the detachment returned to Saigon, their victorious and successful conclusion of the mission did not please the general. In an explosion of brassy anger, Falconi and his guys were kicked out of the south Vietnamese city and put out to pasture in time for a good drenching by the monsoon rains.

The situation was not too bad for everyone concerned. In fact, it turned out to be a pleasant one for Falconi, Sergeant First Class Malpractice McCorckel, and recently promoted Corporal Archie Dobbs. A clinic for the families of the Vietnamese militia unit station at Nui Dep was established under the direction of Lieutenant Andrea Thuy. This beautiful Eurasian lady not only was a member of the Black Eagles herself but also Falconi's lady. Andrea brought two nurses along with her: Second Lieutenant Betty Lou Pemberton, who was Archie Dobbs' girlfriend, and Malpractice's wife Jean. Jean was a Vietnamese whom the Black Eagle medic had met on a previous operation. They'd wasted no time falling in love and getting married.

The presence of these ladies gave the three men a semblance of normalcy in their lives. The other guys bore them no grudge, however, and amused themselves with dalliances among the less morally inclined camp followers who had established themselves at Nui Dep. Which, in actuality, was the same activity they would have been engaged in had General Taggart left them to the delights offered by Saigon's fleshpots.

The Night of the Lutefisk began with the arrival of a package for Sergeant Gunnar Olson. Gunnar, a native of Minnesota, was of Scandinavian ancestry. He received a gift from his folks in Knee Lake, Minnesota, which was a Norwegian food called lutefisk.

Lutefisk was a gelatinous fish that had been treated with a lye solution to preserve it. In the old country—and the American Midwest—those hardy descendants of Vikings prepared the dish by boiling it in cheesecloth, draining it, then covering it with butter before downing the meal with potatoes.

Gunnar loved lutefisk. Since he hadn't been home in nearly two years, he had gone quite a time without eating the stuff. He'd mentioned this fact in a letter home to his mom. Mrs. Olson immediately prepared a large batch of the dish. After packing it in dry ice to ensure nonspoilage on the long trip, she had it special-delivered from Knee Lake to Nui Dep.

When it arrived, Gunnar invited all the Black Eagles—and the three ladies—to join him in a lutefisk supper. Looking for anything to supplement the Ten-In-One rations they had been consuming, they happily accepted. A day-long patrol had been planned for the detachment, but Falconi gave Gunnar a break from it so he could stay back in camp and cook the meal. The three women were scheduled for long hours at the dispensary.

Gunnar, bumming some cheesecloth from the artillery unit at the camp, set to preparing the meal. He filled an iron G.I. with water and set it over a bonfire. When it began to rapidly boil, he carefully lowered the wrapped lutefisk into the cauldron. Next he prepared potatoes in foil and stuck them under the coals of the fire to slowly bake to tender perfection.

The fish cooked slowly, giving off an unusual odor. Gunnar thought it smelled great as he stirred and tended the meal. While breathing in the aroma, memories of snowy Minnesota winters danced through his blond Norwegian head. His reveries were interrupted by the camp sanitation officer. The man, a lieutenant, sniffed and looked around with an expression of irritation on his face.

"Do you people have an open sump over here?" he asked.

Gunnar, puzzled, shook his head. "No, sir."

"Then what's that strange smell?" the officer demanded. He continued looking around.

Gunnar sniffed. "I don't smell nothing but this here lutefisk."

The lieutenant walked over to the pot and looked in. "I didn't know you guys had vehicles assigned to you."

Gunnar shrugged. "We don't, sir."

"Then what the hell are you doing preparing these inner-tube patches?"

"That ain't rubber patches. That's lutefisk," Gunnar said, a bit irritated.

"What the hell is loot-uh-fisk?"

"It's a Norwegian fish dish," Gunnar explained. "It's really delicious."

"You mean Scandinavians eat that stuff?" the officer asked.

"They sure as hell do," Gunnar answered.

"Damn! No wonder those Viking raiders were so mean," the lieutenant said. "You put a cover on that pot."

"Yes, sir," Gunnar said, wondering what the hell the big problem was. He slipped the cover over his cooking, opening it up only to stir the food now and then.

When the meal was finally ready, he put out twelve plates in the eating area of the Black Eagle bunker. Each one held a slab of lutefisk and a baked potato. A can of G.I. butter was in the middle to be spread on to each diner's particular taste. By then the rest of the Black Eagles had returned from the patrol and were plenty hungry. Archie Dobbs had stopped off at the dispensary and brought Andrea, Betty Lou, and Jean along with him. All were more than ready to eat.

Gunnar went up to the door of the bunker. "Come and get it," he called.

The detachment and their three lady guests trooped down to the dining area and sat down. The appearance of Gunnar's culinary efforts were not the most appetizing, but Lieutenant Colonel Falconi

17

himself set the tone for the meal. "By golly, Gunnar, it sure looks like a different sort of feast all right."

Archie Dobbs stared at the slab of white substance on his plate. "It sure does."

"I don't think I've ever seen anything quite like this," Sergeant Major Top Gordon said. He'd been a soldier for many years and had traveled over most of the world. "Of course," he added, "I've never been to Norway."

"Well, Sergeant Major," Gunnar said, "you're in for a hell of a treat." Grinning with delight, the Minnesotan smashed up his baked potato and smeared butter all over it and the lutefisk. Then he started eating. The taste of the dish brought the ethnic side of his psyche to the surface. He sighed and said, *"Deilig!"*

The others dug in. After a couple of bites, the meal came to a complete halt. Gunnar, oblivious to the others, continued to consume his food with great gusto.

Finally, grinning weakly, Falconi said, "I don't think I've ever tasted a food that matches this."

"Me neither," Andrea Thuy said. "This is certainly an unusual way to prepare a fish dish."

Blue Richards, an Alabamian practically raised on catfish, nodded his head. "You don't have to swaller this stuff. You jest stick it in yore mouth and it kinda slides down the gullet, don't it?"

Gunnar looked up and noticed Archie Dobbs staring at his plate. The Minnesotan waved his fork at him. "Eat up, Archie."

Archie shrugged. "Oh, that's okay, Gunnar. I ain't hungry. I ate yesterday."

18

"What we really need," Gunnar said, "is some lefse. I wish my mom had sent some along, but I guess you can't have everything, right?"

"That's right, Gunnar," Ray Swift Elk said. He vaguely wondered if lefse and lutefisk were alike in taste and texture.

But everybody, including Archie, finally finished the meal out of politeness. "I got some more," Gunnar announced. "But I'd like to save it for myself if you don't mind."

"Hell, no, Gunnar!" Malpractice exclaimed. "You just go right ahead and set it aside."

"That's right," Calvin Culpepper said. "We don't want to hog your looty-fisk."

"It's just that I won't be getting it too often," Gunnar explained. "It's real special to me."

"We understand," Falconi said. "That was delicious, Gunnar."

"Yes," Betty Lou said. "Don't you dare give up any of this for us. After all, your mother really meant it for you."

"That's real understanding, folks," Gunnar said gratefully.

Paulo Garcia, who had been a professional fisherman before entering the service, was quizzical. "What do they do to this fish anyhow?"

"It's preserved in lye," Gunnar said. "It's quite a process. Only a Norwegian would be able to come up with such a concept."

"I'll drink to that," Archie Dobbs said.

Betty Lou stood up and took Archie by the arm. "Well! After a meal like that, I could certainly use a walk."

Archie nodded. "Good idea. Thanks again, Gunnar. We'll see you later."

The two lovers walked up the steps of the bunker and stepped out into the now dark outside. Light discipline, because of Viet Cong activity, was strictly enforced within the camp. The moon was bright, however, despite the ominous build-up of clouds off to the south.

"The monsoon is going to be here any day," Archie said. "You can almost smell the moisture in the air."

"I can't smell anything after that lutefisk," Betty Lou said.

They strolled out of the Black Eagle area and into the main camp. "How come you're so anxious for a walk?" Archie asked. He winked at her. "Do you feel romantic?"

Betty Lou shook her head. "We have to have a talk, Archie."

"Okay," he said.

"And I mean a serious one," she added. "Let's go over to the dispensary. It's more private."

Archie leered at her. "Oh, boy!"

"I'm not kidding, Archie," Betty Lou warned him. "We're going to have a real heart-to-heart conversation."

"Uh oh!" he remarked, grimacing. "I wonder what I've done now."

They went through the native militia village that took up the greater part of Nui Dep. Betty Lou received polite greetings from the Vietnamese families who waved at her from the open sides of their thatched huts. The American *v-ta* was well

20

respected by the people for the unselfish medical aid she donated to them—particularly the children.

When they reached the dispensary, they went inside. Archie, knowing that some sort of lecture was going to be delivered, went to the ice machine and got himself a cupful for some cold water. He sat down at Betty's desk and waited to hear what she had to say.

She leaned against a gurney on the other side of the room, her arms folded and the expression on her face serious. "Archie, my tour in Vietnam is up next month."

He nodded. "Yeah?"

"I'll be going to the Letterman in San Francisco," Betty Lou said. "After that I've only a year to go before I'll be released from the Army."

"Well," he said easily. "You're a nurse. You won't have any trouble getting a job."

"How does all this affect you?" she asked.

"Well, if you want to get outta 'Nam, then I'm real happy for you," Archie said. He sipped the water. "Maybe by the time your final discharge comes, we'll have this war wrapped up and the Black Eagles will be sent home."

"This damned war is going to go on forever," Betty Lou said. "Besides, you guys aren't on regular tours like other troops. You've been in Vietnam more than a year yourself."

"Sure," Archie said. "I've been in the Black Eagles a little over two years. We're working for the CIA. Ever'body, including the VC, knows that. And I'm a career military guy like the others. We ain't going home to discharges and vine-covered cottages with

21

the wife and kiddies waiting."

"I want a vine-covered cottage, Archie," Betty Lou said. "I may be a working nurse all my life, but I want a regular home to go to."

"I have thirteen years to go in the Army," Archie said. "We'll be living in rented apartments 'til I retire."

"That almost sounds like a proposal of marriage," Betty Lou said.

Archie sighed. "You're right. We've got to sit down for a long, long talk about us, don't we?"

Betty Lou decided to pull no punches at that point. "Archie, I want you out of the Black Eagles."

"Betty Lou—"

"That's final," she said, going to the door. "You get out of the Black Eagles or we're through."

Archie watched her depart. He sipped the ice water slowly, the ultimatum going through his mind. He had been a member of Lieutenant Colonel Robert Falconi's detachment almost from the beginning. He had joined the unit for its second mission. Being a Black Eagle wasn't a duty assignment, it was a way of life.

Archie fully realized he was going to have to make a decision that would be a heartbreaker one way or the other.

CHAPTER 2

The Black Eagles did not suddenly spring into being. On the other hand, they were not a slowly evolving, old established unit with years of tradition behind them, either.

In reality, they were the brainchild of a Central Intelligence Agency case officer Clayton Andrews. But his creation of the detachment was not an easy process by any means. His initial plans to activate the unit were met with the usual stodgy, stupid resistance that miltary bureaucrats—like all bureaucrats—give to any innovative new ideas. But Clayton Andrews was not the kind of individual to take such mindless rebuffs kindly.

That man growled and bashed his way through knotted red tape for months before he finally received the official okay to turn his concept of creating an independent band of jungle fighters into a living, breathing, ass-kicking reality.

In those early days of the 1960s, "Think Tanks" of Ph.D.'s at various centers of American political thought and study were conducting mental wrestling matches with the problem of fighting communism in southeast Asia. The threat of this ideology spreading in that part of the world was very real indeed. Powerful people in the United States government were concerned enough that some of the best brains in the country were assigned to come up with a solution on containing this political and military force.

Andrews was involved in that same program, but in a much more physical way than the brainy types. His work was in marked contrast to their efforts, his method of handling the situation not intellectual, but purely physical.

He was in combat.

And the CIA man participated in more than just a small amount of shadowy fighting in Cambodia, Laos, and Vietnam. He hit that violent underworld of clandestine killing in a big way. His activities included a hell of a lot of missions that went beyond mere harassment operations in Viet Cong and Pathet Lao areas. His main job was to conduct penetrations into North Vietnam itself. Over a very short period of time this dangerous assignment cost plenty of good men their lives because some of the personnel involved, no matter how dedicated or brave, were not the proper men for such a dangerous undertaking. The appalling casualty rate motivated Andrews to begin his battle with the stodgy military administration to set things up properly.

It took diplomatic persuasion—combined with a few ferocious outbreaks of temper—before the program was eventually expanded. When the final approval was granted, Andrews was suddenly thrust into a position where he needed not simply an *excellent* combat commander, he needed the *best*. Thus, he began an extensive search for an officer to lead the special detachment that would carry out certain down-and-dirty missions that would border on the suicidal.

There were months of personnel investigations and countless interviews with hopeful contenders for the job. In the end, after his exhaustive effort, Andrews settled on a Special Forces captain named Robert Falconi.

Pulling all the strings he could, Andrews saw to it that the Green Beret officer was transferred to his own branch of SOG—the Special Operations Group—to begin work on this brand-new project.

Immediately upon his arrival from his Special Forces detachment, Captain Falconi was tasked with organizing a new fighting unit to be known as the Black Eagles. This group's basic policy was to be primitive and simple. Falconi summed it up in his own words: "Seek out the enemy and kill the sons of bitches."

Their mission was to penetrate deep into the heartland of the communists to disrupt, destroy, maim, and slay. They would also have to accept the fact that giving their own lives might be a requirement of bringing such operations to a successful conclusion. The men of the Black Eagles would be volunteers from every branch of the armed forces. And that was to include all nationalities involved in the struggle against the Red invasion of South Vietnam.

25

Each man was to be an absolute master in his particular brand of military mayhem. He had to be an expert in not only his own nation's firearms but also those of other friendly and enemy countries. But the required knowledge in weaponry didn't stop at the modern types. It also included knives, bludgeons, garrotes, and even crossbows when the need to deal silent death was necessary.

Additionally, there was a requirement for the more sophisticated and peaceful vocations. Foreign languages, land navigation, communications, medical skills, and even mountaineering and scuba diving were to be within the realm of knowledge of the Black Eagles. In addition, each man was to know how to type. In an outfit that had no clerks, this office skill was extremely important because each had to do his own paperwork. Much of this involved the operations orders that directed their highly complicated, dangerous missions. These documents had to be legible and easy to read in order to avoid confusing, deadly errors in combat.

Now it was Falconi who combed through 201-files and called up men for interviews. Some he had served with before, others he knew by reputation, while there were also hundreds whose military records reflected their qualifications. Scores were interviewed, but in the end only a dozen were selected.

They became the enforcement arm of SOG, drawing the missions which were the most dangerous and sensitive. In essence they were hit men, closely coordinated and completely dedicated, held together and directed through the forceful personality of their leader Captain Robert Falconi.

Finally, as with all good men, Clayton Andrews did his work too well. Despite his protests, he was promoted out of the job. Immediately a new CIA officer moved in. Chuck Fagin—an ex-paratrooper and veteran of both World War II and the Korean War—had a natural talent when it came to dreaming up nasty things to do to the unfriendlies up north. It didn't take him long to get Falconi and his boys busy.

Their first efforts were directed against a pleasure palace in North Vietnam.[1] This bordello par excellence was used by communist officials during their retreats from the trials and tribulations of administering authority and regulation over their slave populations. These Red hotshots found that there were no excesses, perverted tastes, or unusual demands that went unsatisfied in this hidden fleshpot.

Falconi and his wrecking crew sky-dived into the operational area in a HALO (High Altitude Low Opening) infiltration, and when the Black Eagles finished their raid on the whorehouse, there was hardly a soul left alive to continue the debauchery.

Their next hell-trek into the enemy's hinterlands was an even more dangerous assignment, with the difficulty factor multiplied by the special demands placed on them.[2] The North Vietnamese had set up a special prison camp in which they were perfecting their skills in the torture-interrogation of downed American pilots. With the conflict escalating in

[1] Black Eagles No. 1—*Hanoi Hellground.*
[2] Black Eagles No. 2—*Mekong Massacre.*

southeast Asia, they rightly predicted they would soon have more than just a few Yanks in their hands. A North Korean brainwashing expert had come over from his native country to teach them the finer points of mental torment. He had learned his despicable trade during the Korean War when he had American POWs directly under his control. His use of psychological torture, combined with just the right amount of physical torment, had broken more than one man despite the most spirited resistance. Experts who studied his methods came to the conclusion that only a completely insane prisoner, whose craziness caused him to abandon both the sensation of pain and the instinct for survival, could have resisted the North Korean's methods.

At the time of the Black Eagles' infiltration into North Vietnam, the prisoners behind the barbed wire were few—but important. A U.S.A.F. pilot, an Army Special Forces sergeant, and two high-ranking officers of the South Vietnamese forces were the unwilling tenants of the concentration camp.

Falconi and his men not only were tasked to rescue the POWs but they also had to bring along the prison's commandant and his North Korean tutor. Falconi pulled off the job, fighting his way south through the North Vietnamese Army and Air Force to a bloody showdown on the Song Bo River. The situation deteriorated to the point that the Black Eagles' magazines had their last few rounds in them as they waited for the NVA's final charge. The unexpected but spirited aid from anticommunist guerrillas turned the tide, and the Black Eagles smashed their way out of the encirclement.

The next operation took them to Laos where they were pitted against the fanatical savages of the Pathet Lao.[3] If that wasn't bad enough, their method of entrance into the operational area was bizarre and dangerous. This type of transport into battle hadn't been used in active combat in more than twenty years. It had even been labeled obsolete by military experts. But this didn't deter the Black Eagles.

They used a glider to make a silent flight to a secret landing zone. To make a bad situation worse, the operations plan called for their extraction through a glider-recovery apparatus that not only hadn't been tested in combat, but had never been given sufficient trial under rehearsed, safe conditions.

After a hairy ride in the flimsy craft, they hit the ground to carry out a mission designed to destroy the construction site of a Soviet nuclear power plant the Reds wanted to install in the area. Everything went wrong from the start, and the Black Eagles fought against a horde of insane zealots until their extraction to safety. This was completely dependent on the illegal and unauthorized efforts of a dedicated U.S.A.F. pilot—the same one they had rescued from the North Vietnam prison camp. The Air Force colonel was determined to help the same men who had saved him, and he came through with all pistons firing, paying the debt he owed Falconi's guys.

This hairy episode was followed by two occurrences: the first was Captain Robert Falconi's

[3] Black Eagles No. 3—*Nightmare in Laos.*

promotion to major, and the second was a mission that was doubly dangerous because it was impossible to make firm operation plans. Unknown Caucasian personnel, posing as U.S. troops, had been committing atrocities against Vietnamese peasants.[4] The situation had gotten far enough out of control that the effectiveness of American efforts in the area had been badly damaged. Once again Falconi and the Black Eagles were called in to put things right. They went in on a dark beach from a submarine and began a determined reconnaissance until they finally made contact with their quarry.

These enemy agents, wearing U.S. Army uniforms, were dedicated East German communists prepared to fight to the death for their cause. The Black Eagles admired such unselfish dedication to the extent that they gave the Reds the opportunity to accomplish that end: sacrifice their lives for communism.

But this mission wasn't successfully concluded without the situation deteriorating to the point the Black Eagles had to endure human wave assaults from a North Vietnamese Army battalion led by an infuriated general. This officer had been humiliated by Falconi on the Song Bo River several months previously. The mission ended in another Black Eagle victory, but not before five more good men had died.

Brought back to Saigon at last, the seven survivors of the previous operations cleaned their weapons, drew fresh, clean uniforms, and prepared

4 Black Eagles No. 4—*Pungi Patrol.*

30

for a long-awaited period of R&R—Rest and Recreation.

It was not to be.

Chuck Fagin's instincts and organization of agents had ferreted out information that showed a high-ranking intelligence officer of the South Vietnamese army had been leaking information on the Black Eagles to his superiors up in the Communist North.[5] It would have been easy enough to arrest this double agent; however, an entire enemy espionage net had been involved. Thus, Falconi and his Black Eagles had to come in from the boondocks to fight the good fight against these spies and assassins in the back streets of Saigon itself.

When Saigon was relatively cleaned up, the Black Eagles drew a mission that involved going out on the Ho Chi Minh Trail over which the North Vietnamese sent supplies, weapons, and munitions south to be used by the Viet Cong and elements of the North Vietnamese Army.[5] The enemy was enjoying great success despite repeated aerial attacks by the U.S. and South Vietnamese air forces. The high command decided that only a sustained campaign conducted on the ground would put a crimp in the Reds' operation.

Naturally, they chose the Black Eagles for the dirty job.

Falconi and his men waged partisan warfare in its most primitive and violent fashion with raids, ambushes, and other forms of jungle fighting. The

[5] Black Eagles No. 5—*Saigon Slaughter*.
[6] Black Eagles No. 6—*Ak47 Firefight*.

31

order of the day was "kill or be killed," as the monsoon forest thundered with reports of numerous types of modern weaponry. This dangerous situation was made even more deadly by a decidedly insidious and deadly form of mine warfare which made each track and trail through the brush a potential zone of death.

When this was wrapped up, Falconi and his troops received an even bigger assignment. This next operation involved working with Chinese mercenaries to secure an entire province ablaze with infiltration and invasion by the North Vietnamese Army.[7] This even involved beautiful Andrea Thuy, a lieutenant in the South Vietnamese Army who had been attached to the Black Eagles. Playing on the mercenaries' superstitions and religion, she became a "warrior-sister," leading some of the blazing combat herself.

An affair of honor followed this mission, when Red agents kidnapped this lovely woman.[8] They took her north—but not for long. Falconi and the others pulled a parachute-borne attack and brought her out of the hellhole where her communist tormentors had put her.

The ninth mission, pulled off with most of the detachment's veterans away on R&R, involved a full-blown attack by North Vietnamese regulars into the II Corps area—all this while saddled with a pushy newspaper reporter.[9]

By that time South Vietnam had rallied quite a

[7] Black Eagles No. 7—*Beyond the DMZ.*
[8] Black Eagles No. 8—*Boocoo Death.*
[9] Black Eagles No. 9—*Bad Scene at Bong Son.*

number of allies to her side. Besides the United States, there was South Korea, Australia, New Zealand, the Philippines, and Thailand. This situation upset the communist side, and they decided to counter it by openly having various Red countries send contingents of troops to bolster the NVA (North Vietnamese Army) and the Viet Cong.

This resulted in a highly secret situation—ironically well known by both the American and communist sides—which developed in the borderland between Cambodia and South Vietnam.[10] The Reds, in an effort to make their war against the Americans a truly international struggle, began an experimental operation involving volunteers from Algeria. These young Arab communists, led by hardcore Red officers, were to be tested against U.S. troops. If they proved effective, other nationalities would be brought in from behind the Iron Curtain to expand the insurgency against the Americans, South Vietnamese, and their allies.

Because of the possibility of failure, the Reds did not want to publicize these "volunteers" to the conflict unless the experiment proved a rousing success. The American brass also did not want the situation publicized under any circumstances. To do so would be to play into the world-opinion manipulations of the communists.

But the generals in Saigon wanted the situation neutralized as quickly as possible.

Thus, Falconi and the Black Eagles moved into the jungle to take on the Algerians, led by fanatical Major Omar Ahmed. Ahmed, who rebelled against

[10] Black Eagles No. 10—*Cambodia Kill Zone.*

France in Algeria, had actually fought in the French Army in Indochina as an enemy of the very people he ended up serving. Captured before the Battle of Dien Bien Phu, he had been an easy and pliable subject for the Red brainwashers and interrogators. When he returned to his native Algeria after repatriation, he was a dedicated communist ready to take on anything the free world could throw at him.

Falconi and his men, with their communication system destroyed by deceit, fought hard. But they were badly outnumbered and finally forced into a situation where their backs were literally pinned against the wall of a jungle cliff. But Archie Dobbs, injured on the infiltration jump and evacuated from the mission back to the U.S. Army hospital at Long Binh, went AWOL in order to rejoin his buddies in combat. He not only successfully returned to them, but arrived in a helicopter gunship that threw in the fire support necessary to turn the situation around.

The communist experiment was swept away in the volleys of aerial fire and the final bayonet charge of the Black Eagles. The end result was a promotion to lieutenant colonel for Robert Falconi while his senior non-coms also were given a boost up the Army's career ladder. Archie Dobbs, who had gone AWOL from the hospital, was demoted in spite of his heroic act.

After Operation Cambodian Challenge, the Black Eagles only received the briefest of rests back at their base garrison. This return to Camp Nui Dep with fond hopes of R& R dancing through their combat-buzzed minds was interrupted by the next challenge to their courage and ingenuity. This was a mission

34

that was dubbed Operation Song Cai Duel.[11]

Communist patrol boats had infiltrated the Song Cai River and controlled that waterway north of Dak Bla. Their activities ranged from actual raiding of river villages and military outposts to active operations involving the transportation and infiltration of Red agents.

This campaign resulted in the very disturbing fact that the Song Cai River, though in South Vietnam, was under the complete control of Ho Chi Minh's fighters. They virtually owned the waterway.

The brass's orders to Falconi were simple: *Get the river back!*

The mission, however, was much more complicated. Distances were long, and logistics and personnel were not in the quantities needed. But that had never stopped the Black Eagle detachment before.

There were new lessons to be learned, too. River navigation, powerboating, and amphibious warfare had to be added to the Black Eagles' skills in jungle fighting.

Outgunned and outnumbered, Falconi and his guys waded in over their heads. The pressure mounted to the point that the village they used as a base headquarters had to be evacuated. But a surprise appearance by Chuck Fagin with a couple of quad-fifty machine guns turned the tide.

The final showdown was a gunboat battle that turned the muddy waters of the Song Cai red with blood.

It was pure hell for the men, but it was another

[11] Black Eagles No. 11—*Duel on the Song Cai.*

brick laid in the wall of their brief and glorious history.

The next Black Eagle adventure began on a strange note. A French intelligence officer, who was a veteran of France's Indochinese War, was attached to SOG in an advisory role. While visiting the communications room, he was invited to listen in on an intermittent radio transmission in the French language that the section had been monitoring for several months. When he heard it, the Frenchman was astounded. The broadcast was from a French soldier who correctly identified himself through code as a member of the G.M.I. (*Groupement Mixte d'Intervention*), which had been carrying on guerrilla warfare using native volunteers in the old days.[12]

Contact was made, and it was learned that this Frenchman was indeed a G.M.I. veteran who had been reported missing in action during mountain insurgency operations in 1953. And he'd done more than just survive for fifteen years. He was the leader of a large group of Meo tribesmen who were actively raiding into North Vietnam from Laos.

The information was kicked "upstairs" and the brass hats became excited. Not only was this man a proven ass-kicker, but he could provide valuable intelligence and an effective base of operations to launch further missions into the homeland of the Reds. It was officially decided to make contact with the man and bring him into the "Big Picture" by supplying him with arms, equipment, and money to continue his war against the communists. The G3

[12] Black Eagles No. 12—*Lord of Laos*.

Section also thought it would be a great idea to send in a detachment of troops to work with him.

They chose Lieutenant Colonel Robert Falconi and his Black Eagles for the job.

But when the detachment infiltrated the operational area they did not find a dedicated anticommunist. Instead, they were faced with an insane French Army sergeant named Farouche who reigned over an opium empire high in the Laotian mountains. He had contacted the allies only for added weaponry and money in his crazy plans to wrest power from other warlords.

The mission dissolved into sheer hell. Falconi and the guys not only had to travel by foot back through five hundred miles of enemy territory to reach the safety of friendly lines. To make the trip a bit more interesting, they also had to fight both the communists and Farouche's tribesmen every step of the way.

The effort cost them three good men, and when they finally returned to safety, Archie Dobbs found that his nurse sweetheart had left him for another man. Enraged and broken-hearted, the detachment scout took off on another AWOL escapade, this time to track down his lady love and her new boyfriend.

Falconi also expanded his Table of Organization and built up another fire team to give the detachment a grand total of three. Ray Swift Elk was commissioned an officer and made second in command, Sergeant Major Top Gordon was released from the hospital, and Malpractice McCorckel and Calvin Culpepper returned from furlough.

Six new men were added to the roster, so despite Archie Dobbs' disappearance, the detachment was in damned good shape numerically.

They didn't have long to sit back and enjoy their condition. Their next adventure came on them hard and fast after the Soviet Union had constructed a high-powered communications center in North Vietnam with the capability of monitoring and jamming satellite transmissions.[13] The project had been so secretive that it was a long while before western intelligence heard about it. Its location was hazardous for potential attackers. There were several strong military posts in the vicinity, and the area had a heavy concentration of population.

Like they said at SOG headquarters: "Only madmen or the Black Eagles would attempt to destroy the site."

Falconi was charged with infiltrating the area, blowing up the target, then getting the hell out of there. The latter part was a big problem, and the colonel came up with a bizarre exfiltration scheme. He planned to add insult to injury by meeting an aircraft on the reconstructed air strip at Dien Bien Phu that had been rebuilt as a tourist site.

The Black Eagles had an asset who met them on their initial entry into the operational area. This person was born and raised in the area and knew every nook and cranny of the terrain. The agent's identity was kept secret until the last possible moment, and Falconi's usual calm demeanor was sorely tested when he found himself working with Andrea Thuy—his former sweetheart from the de-

[13] Black Eagles 13—*Encore at Dien Bien Phu.*

tachment's "old days."

Despite emotional and tactical problems, Falconi directed a successful mission. The huge communications complex was blown to hell, and the aircraft was met for the escape after a few hectic hours of evading enemy troops.

The Black Eagle adventure that followed all this was instigated by the sensitivity and hurt feelings of a Soviet officer.[14] Lieutenant Colonel Gregori Krashchenko of the Russian KGB had been humiliated once too often by Robert Falconi and his Black Eagles. The Soviet spy's superiors agreed and gave him unlimited authority to get back at the Americans who had been kicking ass in Vietnam.

Krashchenko had very definite ideas of how to defeat an elite unit: form up a similar outfit of his own! Thus, he spent six months whipping together the Soviet version of the Black Eagles. This group of dedicated communists had been carefully recruited out of the ranks of the Soviet Union's most elite forces—the paratroops, naval infantry, and even specially trained scouts and trackers of the KGB Border Guard. In the spirit of international communism, there were also some handpicked specialists from various Iron Curtain nations. This group, whom Krashchenko named the Red Bears, went through a brutally tough training program designed to whip them into shape to meet Falconi's men in the jungles of Vietnam.

Krashchenko was not fooling when he set his standards. He wanted the best and he made damned sure he got the cream of the crop. Of the one

[14] Black Eagles No. 14—*Rang Dong Challenge.*

hundred and fifty men who volunteered for the Red Bears, only sixteen made the grade. These proved themselves to be the toughest of the tough as far as communist militarism went. Dedicated to the idea of seeking out and destroying Falconi's Black Eagles, these zealots were armed with the latest weaponry and carried the best equipment. There was nothing they lacked in support from the Soviet High Command.

Completely outfitted and insane with a fighting desire, they were ready to be wound up and turned loose. The KGB notified their counterparts in the CIA of the Red Bears and threw down the gauntlet of challenge: If Falconi and his men had the balls, they'd find seventeen bad-ass Reds waiting for them in the jungle vicinity where the international borders of North Vietnam, South Vietnam, and Cambodia met.

The C.I.A. carefully considered the dare given them. There was more at stake here than a simple test of wills and pride. The entire intelligence community of the world would be watching. The prestige—and, consequently, effectiveness in re-cruiting and operations—of each side was part of the big pot to be won.

Thus, the challenge was accepted and Falconi took sixteen of his hardest hitting vets in with him for this Asian showdown, where only the quick and deadly woud survive.

The fighting was horrific and bloody, and did not end until the Red Bears and their crazed commander were wiped out, and eight of Falconi's men—half his command—had also given the ultimate sacrifice for their cause. They returned from the field, mauled but proud, and Chuck Fagin saw to it they got a few weeks off to get their heads back together.

After that bloody encounter, Lieutenant Colonel Robert Falconi pared down the Black Eagles and gave the detachment a "mean and lean" look. That streamlining was necessary for their next assignment.

There were too many infiltration trails into South Vietnam. The Reds thought they could waltz into their illegal operational areas as they damned well pleased. They even went so far as to establish rest areas and training camps in territories where American armed forces and their allies should have held complete control.

The next mission was to enter the affected area for a lengthy operation of intimidation and harassment.[15] The Black Eagles had to live off the land and steal from their enemies between rare parachute supply drops. That meant almost going native and turning from soldiers into warriors in the green hell of the jungle.

But, unknown to the brass in Saigon at the time, some of the best units of the North Vietnamese Army were scheduled to move into that same contested territory to prepare for a major offensive.

Falconi and his men found themselves between the proverbial "rock and the hard place." Completely surrounded and overwhelmingly outnumbered, Falconi was too damned mad and proud to pull a retreat.

Even after Brigadier General James Taggart

[15] Black Eagles No. 15—*Uncle Ho's Hellhounds.*

ordered the Black Eagles to withdraw, Falconi would not leave. Too many good men had given up the ghost in worse situations. It seemed like a betrayal of their memory to cut and run. The lieutenant colonel radioed back to Saigon that he would hold until relieved or wiped out. The detachment not only held, but managed to bring out some Vietnamese peasants trapped within the communist forces.

But Taggart didn't like being disobeyed, so he banished the Black Eagles from their Saigon billets back to the boondocks of Nui Dep.

It is to the Black Eagles' credit that unit integrity and morale always seemed to increase despite the staggering losses they suffered. Not long after their initial inception, the detachment decided they wanted an insignia all their own. This wasn't at all unusual for units in Vietnam. Local manufacturers, acting on designs submitted to them by the troops involved, produced these emblems that were worn by the outfits while "in country." These adornments were strictly nonregulation and unauthorized for display outside of Vietnam.

Falconi's men came up with a unique beret badge manufactured as a cloth insignia. A larger version was used as a shoulder patch. The design consisted of a black eagle—naturally—with spread wings. The big bird's beak was opened in a defiant battle cry, and he clutched a sword in one claw and a bolt of lightning in the other. Mounted on a khaki shield that was trimmed in black, the device was an accurate portrayal of its wearers: somber and deadly.

The Black Eagles, because of the secret nature of their existence, were not always able to sport the insignia. But when they could, the men wore it with great pride.

There was one more touch of their individuality that they kept to themselves. It was a motto which not only worked as a damned good password in hairy situations, but also described the Black Eagles' basic philosophy.

Those special words, in Latin, were: *CALCITRA CLUNIS!*

This phrase, in the language of the ancient Roman legionnaires who served Julius Caesar, translated as: KICK ASS!

CHAPTER 3

The most notorious season of weather known to man is called the monsoon by Asian natives and visitors alike. The name comes from the Arabic word *mausim,* which means "season."

When speaking of that particular time of the year, people refer to the endless rains. But the wetness is only one portion of the weather. The wind direction is just as important, for it dictates the actual conditions. In southeast Asia the prevailing winds in the summer are southwesterly, while those of winter are northeasterly. It is those winds traveling southwest that bring the drenching torrents of rain that sweep across the continent in yearly cycles.

A few weeks after the Black Eagles arrived in Camp Nui Dep, those moisture-bearing winds kicked up their season patterns. At first there were just a few warning showers that went away to be replaced by hot sunshine. But the rainfall became more and more prevalent until, finally, the splashing torrents rolled across the land turning open areas into quagmires and the heavily vegetated regions into wet, dripping badlands.

The routine at Nui Dep slowed to a crawl. Only a few patrols went out into the saturated jungle, where they found nothing remarkable to report back. They returned to the camp soaked and chilly, looking forward to hot coffee and heated C-ration meals.

When the monsoon swung into full strength and the rain really started pouring down, all operations came to a halt. Planes and choppers were grounded, and the small garrison with its fortified village of native militia settled in for a damp wait. Card games, beer drinking, war stories, and other amusements passed the slow, soggy hours.

It looked like a long, dreary, sopping monsoon with plenty of boredom and quiet.

Ngoyen Li, a battalion commander in the Viet Cong, was an old campaigner. He'd fought the Japanese on the French side, the French on the Viet Minh side, and now fought the Americans on the Viet Cong side. A tough, wiry old bastard, his carcass was covered with the scars of countless campaigns.

A wedge-shaped, thick mark showed where a Japanese infrantryman had driven his sixteen-inch bayonet into Ngoyen, then twisted it. The wound had been massive, but now the Japanese infantryman was no more than scattered bones in the jungle. The Vietnamese had wrenched himself loose from the blade, then charged his attacker in a mad rage, choking him to death. Other scars were made by bullets of a half dozen different calibers. These were intertwined by marks left from the shrapnel of numerous artillery and mortar shells. A few toes were missing on his right foot when a badly planted mine he'd stepped on blew downward instead of upward like it should have.

Battalion Commander Ngoyen Li lived for combat. His entire life, after all the years of pain and strife, was dedicated to doing battle. Although a member of the Communist Party, the officer was actually more devoted to fighting than to any political ideology. Neither hardship, pain, hunger, thirst, fatigue, or other physical discomfort was taken into consideration by Ngoyen Li when he went into battle.

Now, in the heavy rainfall splattering down through the tall jungle trees, he stood soaking wet, yelling orders at his struggling soldiers. *"Di thang day! Mau len!* Move ahead, quickly!"

The guerrillas, laboring through the thick mud under the heavy loads on their backs and shoulders, pushed ahead with renewed vigor despite exhaustion and mental fatigue. They had begun this long journey weeks before in dry weather. The going had been tough enough then in the high humidity and temperatures of the jungle. But at least the footing on the narrow trails had been firm and solid. But for the previous several days, they had struggled through soft mud, sinking in past their ankles while traveling slowly and painfully forward with their heavy loads.

But none of those dedicated Viet Cong complained. They revered Ngoyen Li. He was a living legend of bravery and fierceness, and all tried to live up to his high standards.

The young guerrilla smiled up at him, forgetting the crushing weight of the M1937 Russian mortars they bore on their spindly bodies. All knew they were a part of a grand battle scheme that would bring a great victory from the unsuspecting Americans they sought to attack.

A lieutenant, rainwater running off his pith helmet, forced his way through the thick palm fronds until he reached his commander. "Comrade Battalion Commander Ngoyen Li!" he called out.

The old campaigner turned to see who had called him. He displayed a gap-toothed grin at the young officer. Ngoyen Li liked the youngster's spunk. "Yes, Nam?"

"I have an exact fix on our position," Nam announced.

"*Tot!*" Ngoyen Li exclaimed. "Let's get under the tree and have a look."

The two got out of the direct rain. Nam spread out the Chinese map he carried in a waterproof pouch slung over his shoulder. "I shot six different azimuths from the top of a tall tree, Comrade Battalion Commander," he said.

Ngoyen Li looked carefully at him. "Is that how you got those scratches on your arms, Comrade Platoon Leader?"

Nam nodded sheepishly. "*Co.* I started to fall on my way down and had to grab on hard. The bark was very sharp."

"Have the medics put *canh-ki-dot* on those," Ngoyen Li said. "They are deep and wide."

48

The lieutenant shrugged. "They are nothing, Comrade Battalion Commander."

"It is easy to get an infection during this dirty, wet weather," Ngoyen Li reminded him. "A man wounded during the monsoon faces death much more than one who falls in the dry season."

"Yes, Comrade Battalion Commander. I will see the medics," Nam said. He pointed to an X he'd drawn on the map. "This is where we are at this moment."

Ngoyen Li reached into his jacket pocket and retrieved a small plastic case. He opened it and pulled out a pair of spectacles. After putting them on, he studied the map in the weak light. "Mmm," he mused. "Yes—yes—we have come five kilometers since yesterday."

Nam glanced out at the trail where the soldiers walked past in a single-file column. Every man had some sort of extra load besides his own gear. The lieutenant looked back at his commander. "Comrade Battalion Commander, the men do not complain of the hard task you have set for them. But as an officer I must advise you that their strength is waning rapidly."

Ngoyen Li nodded. "I realize that, Comrade Platoon Leader. But we are not far from our objective." He placed his finger on the exact spot. "There!"

Nam read the name there. "Nui Dep?"

"Yes," Ngoyen Li said. "Nui Dep."

The rain splattered heavily down on the rows of

49

sandbags placed on top of the Black Eagle's bunker. This protection, six layers deep, sat heavy and solid on the sheet-iron roof.

Inside, under the weak illumination of a hissing G.I. gasoline lantern, five serious men concentrated on the undertaking they'd set themselves to that afternoon.

"I'll bet a dollar," Paulo Garcia said.

Malpractice McCorckel didn't hesitate. "I'll see that dollar and go you fifty cents more."

"Easy money," Paulo said, throwing in another half a buck.

Blue Richards grinned easily. "Y'all boys make it tough for a poor ol' country feller like me." But he bet a dollar fifty to stay in the game.

Calvin "Buffalo Soldier" Culpepper laughed. "Now we're gonna play some real poker. I'll see that dollar and a half and go another dollar and a half." He looked at Gunnar. "Three to you, my man."

"Yeah," Paulo said, paying up. "And don't try to bet none of that lutefisk."

"Jeez," Gunnar said. "Sometimes I think you guys didn't like that meal." He threw his cards in. "Anyhow. I'm out."

Calvin looked over at Malpractice. "Well? You in or out?"

"I'm thinking," Malpractice said pensively, studying his cards.

Calvin's laughter increased. "The man has to think before he gives me all his money."

"You're a bluffing sonofabitch," Malpractice said softly. He tossed in the right amount. "We've paid to see, Calvin. Show us your stuff."

50

"Read 'em and weep," Calvin intoned the old saying. He showed a full house—queens over tens.

"Shit!" said Paulo.

"Shit!" said Malpractice.

"Shit!" said Blue.

"Glad I folded," Gunnar said.

The pot, built up from the game of seven card stud, was ten dollars. Calvin swept in his winnings with his big hands. He glanced over at the door where Archie stood staring out into the rain. "Hey, Archie! C'mon man! I need some o' your money."

Archie, saying nothing, continued looking at the water splattering out in the compound.

"Archie," Blue said. "Are you deaf or somethin'?"

"Huh?"

"What the hell's the matter with you?" Paulo asked. "You been real strange lately."

"Stranger'n usual, anyhow," Gunnar added.

"I'm okay, guys," Archie said.

"Want to play poker with us, Archie?" Malpractice asked.

"No thanks. I'm going for a walk," Archie said, going over to his bunk to fetch his poncho.

"A walk! There's a goddamned monsoon out there, you dumbass," Calvin said.

"That's okay," Archie said. He slipped the covering over his head. After arranging it, he went up the steps and stepped out into the muddy ground. He could see the other bunkers scattered throughout Nui Dep. The airfield, usually busy as hell during the dry season, was now a virtual lake. It was completely useless to aircraft, and all had been flown back to Saigon when the rainy season first turned serious.

51

Archie walked through the mud and went to the headquarters bunker. He stomped down the stairs and walked inside. "Hi ya," he said.

Lieutenant Colonel Robert Falconi, Lieutenant Ray Swift Elk, and Sergeant Major Top Gordon looked up from their paperwork chores. Falconi frowned in puzzlement at the unexpected appearance of the detachment scout. "What's up, Archie?"

"Nothing, sir," Archie said, joining them around the desk. He settled down on an empty chair. "How's it going?"

"Pretty good," Top Gordon answered. "We've just about got everyone's 201-file up to snuff."

"Good," Archie said. "Too bad we don't rate a clerk in this outfit, huh?"

"Yeah," Ray Swift Elk said with a meaningful glance at Archie. "And it's too damned bad nobody volunteers to help with the administrative paperwork around here."

"Hey," Archie said in mild protest. "It's all I can do in working up an annex on the OPLANS, sirs."

"At least your heart is in the right place," Top said insincerely. "Is there something you want or are you simply here to dazzle us with your shining personality?"

"Well," Archie said a bit hesitantly. "Actually, I got a question for the colonel."

"Sure, Archie," Falconi said. "Fire away."

"Sir, how long do you think this here war we're in is gonna last?"

Falconi was thoughtful for a few long moments. "I don't really know. We don't have any historical references on this situation. The French fought here

52

from '48 until '54."

"Do you think we might wrap the thing up in another year?" Archie inquired.

"We could wrap it up tomorrow if they'd turn us loose, Archie," Falconi said. "It all depends on the government at home."

"Damn it," Archie said. "If we ain't gonna go for a win, why don't they just knock it off and we'll all go home."

Top frowned. "What the hell is your problem, soldier?"

"Nothing," Archie said. He stood up. "I'll see you later."

Falconi, worried, watched Archie leave. "There's more there than shows on the surface."

Ray Swift Elk agreed. "I think our boy has woman trouble, sir."

Falconi got up and walked to the bunker door. He looked out and saw Archie's forlorn figure trudging through the rain. The lieutenant colonel knew he had a troubled man, and when that situation occurred, it bothered him, too.

CHAPTER 4

Robert Mikhailovich Falconi was born an Army brat at Fort Meade, Maryland, in the year 1934.

His father, Second Lieutenant Michael Falconi, was the son of Italian immigrants. The parents, Salvatore and Luciana Falconi, had wasted no time in instilling appreciation of America and the opportunities offered by the nation into the youngest son. They had already instilled deep patriotism into their seven other children. Mister Falconi even went as far as naming his son Michael rather than the Italian Michele. The boy had been born an American, was going to live as an American so—*per Dio e tutti i santi*—he was going to be named as an American!

Young Michael was certainly no disappointment to his parents or older brothers and sisters. He studied hard in school and excelled. He worked in the family's small shoe repair shop in New York City's Little Italy during the evenings, doing his homework late at night. When he graduated from high school, Michael was eligible for several scholarships to continue his education in college, but even with this help, it would have entailed great sacrifice on the part of his parents. Two older brothers, beginning promising careers as lawyers, could have helped out a bit, but Michael didn't want to be any more of a burden on his family than was absolutely necessary.

He knew of an alternative. The nation's service academies, West Point and Annapolis, offered free education to qualified young men. Michael, through the local ward boss, received a congressional appointment to take the examinations to attend the United States Military Academy.

He was successful in this endeavor and was appointed to the Corps of Cadets. West Point didn't give a damn about his humble origins. It didn't matter to the academy whether his parents were poor immigrants or not. West Point also considered Cadet Michael Falconi as socially acceptable as anyone in the corps regardless of the fact that his father was a struggling cobbler. The only thing that concerned the institution was whether he, as an individual, could cut it or not. It was this measuring of a man by no other standards than his own abilities and talents that caused the young plebe to develop a sincere, lifelong love for the United States Army. He finished his career at the school in the upper third of his class, sporting the three chevrons and rockers of a brigade adjutant upon graduation.

Second Lieutenant Falconi was assigned to the Third Infantry Regiment at Fort Meade, Maryland. This unit was a ceremonial outfit that provided details for military funerals at Arlington National Cemetery, the guard for the Tomb of the Unknown Soldier, and other official functions in the Washington, D.C., area.

The young shavetail enjoyed the bachelor's life in the nation's capital, and his duties as protocol officer, though not too demanding, were interesting. He was required to be present during social occasions that were official ceremonies of state. He coordinated the affairs and saw to it that all the political bigwigs and other brass attending them had a good time. He was doing exactly those duties at such a function when he met a young Russian Jewish refugee named Miriam Ananova Silberman.

She was a pretty, twenty-year-old brunette, who had the most striking eyes that Michael Falconi had ever seen. He would always say throughout his life that it was her eyes that captured his heart. When he met her, Miriam was a member of the League of Jewish Refugees, attending a congressional dinner. She and her father, Rabbi Josef Silberman, had recently fled the Red dictator Stalin's anti-Semitic terrorism in the Soviet Union. Her organization had been lobbying the American Congress to enact legislation that would permit the U.S. government to take action in saving European and Asian Jewry not only from the savagery of the communists but also from the Nazis in Germany, who had only just begun their own program of intimidation and harassment of their country's Jewish population.

When the lieutenant met the refugee beauty at the start of the evening's activities, he fell hopelessly in love. He spent that entire evening as close to her as he possibly could, while ignoring his other duties. A couple of congressmen who arrived late had to scurry around looking for their tables without aid. Lieutenant Falconi's full attention was on Miriam. He was absolutely determined he would get better acquainted with this beautiful Russian. He begged her to dance with him at every opportunity, was solicitous about seeing to her refreshments, and engaged her in conversation, doing his best to be witty and interesting.

He was successful.

Miriam Silberman was fascinated by this tall, dark, and most handsome young officer. She was so swept off her feet that she failed to play the usual coquettish little games employed by most women. His infectious smile and happy charm completely captivated the young belle.

The next day Michael began a serious courtship, determined to win her heart and marry the girl.

Josef Silberman, her father, was a cantankerous, elderly widower. He opposed the match from the beginning. As a Talmud scholar he wanted his only daughter to marry a nice Jewish boy. But Miriam took pains to point out to him that this was America—a country that existed in direct opposition to homogeneous customs. The mixing of nationalities and religions was not that unusual in this part of the world. The rabbi argued, stormed, forbade, and demanded—but all for naught. In the end, so he would not lose the affection of his daughter, he gave his blessing. The couple was married in a nonreligious ceremony at the Fort Meade Post Chapel.

A year later their only child, a son, was born. He was named Robert Mikhailovich.

The boy spent his youth on various army posts. There were only two times he lived in a town or civilian neighborhood. The first was during the years his father, by then a colonel, served overseas in the European Theater of Operations in the First Infantry Division—the Big Red One. A family joke developed out of the colonel's service in that particular outfit. Robert would ask his dad, "Why are you serving in the First Division?"

The colonel always answered, "Because I figured if I was going to be One, I might as well be a Big Red One."

It was one of those private family jokes that don't go over too well outside the home.

The second stint of civilian living was in San Diego, California, during the time that the colonel was assigned as the supervisor of that city's public school Reserve Officer Training Program.

But despite this overabundance of martial neighborhoods, the boy had a happy childhood. The only problem was his dislike of school. Too many genes of ancient Hebrew warriors and Roman legionnaires danced through the youth's fiery soul. Robert was a kid who liked action, adventure, and plenty of it. The only serious studying he ever did was in the karate classes he took when the family was stationed in Japan. He was accepted in one of that island nation's most prestigious martial arts academies where he excelled while evolving in a serious and skillful *karateka*.

His use of this fighting technique caused one of

59

the ironies in his life. In the early 1950s, during the time his father headed up San Diego, California's high school ROTC program, Robert was himself a student—a most indifferent scholar at best. Always looking for excitement, his natural boldness got him into a run-in with some young Mexican-Americans. One of the Chicanos had never seen such devastation as that which Bobby Falconi dealt out with his hands. But the Latin-American kid hung in there, took his lumps, and finally went down when several skillfully administered and lightning-quick *shuto* chops slapped consciousness from his enraged mind.

A dozen years later, this same young gang member named Manuel Rivera once again met Robert Falconi. Rivera was a Special Forces sergeant first class and Falconi a captain in the same elite outfit. SFC Manuel Rivera, a Black Eagle, was killed in action during the raid on the prison camp in North Vietnam in 1964. His name is now listed on the Black Eagles Roll of Honor.

When Falconi graduated from high school in 1952, he immediately enlisted in the Army. Although his father had wanted him to opt for West Point, the young man couldn't stand the thought of being stuck in any more classrooms. In fact, he didn't even want to be an officer. During his early days on army posts he had developed several friendships among career noncommissioned officers. He liked the attitude of these rough-and-tumble professional soldiers who drank, brawled, and fornicated with wild abandon during their off-duty time. The sergeants' devil-may-care attitude seemed much more attractive to young Robert than

60

the heavy responsibilities that seemed to make commissioned officers and their lives so serious and, at times, tedious.

After basic and advanced infantry training, he was shipped straight into the middle of the Korean War where he was assigned to the tough Second Infantry Division.

Falconi participated in two campaigns there. These were designated by the United States Army as: *Third Korean Winter* and *Korean Summer–Fall 1953*. Robert Falconi fought, roasted, and froze in those turbulent months. His combat experience ranged from holding a hill during massive attacks by crazed Chinese communist forces, to the deadly cat-and-mouse activities of night patrols in enemy territory.

He returned stateside with a sergeancy, the Combat Infantryman's Badge, the Purple Heart, the Silver Star, and the undeniable knowledge that he had been born and bred for just one life—that of a soldier.

His martial ambitions also had expanded. He now desired a commission but didn't want to sink himself into the curriculum of the United States Military Academy. His attitude toward schoolbooks remained the same—to hell with 'em!

At the end of his hitch in 1956, he reenlisted and applied for Infantry Officers' Candidate School at Fort Benning, Georgia.

Falconi's time in OCS registered another success in his life. He excelled in all phases of the rigorous course. He recognized the need for work in the classrooms and soaked up the lessons through long hours of study while burning the midnight oil of infantry academia in quarters. The field exercises were a piece of cake for this combat veteran, but he was surprised to find out that, even with his war experience, the instructors had plenty to teach him.

His only setback occurred during "Fuck Your Buddy Week." That was a phase of the curriculum in which the candidates learned responsibility. Each man's conduct—or misconduct—was passed on to an individual designated as his buddy. If a candidate screwed up he wasn't punished. His buddy was. Thus, for the first time in many of these young men's lives, their personal conduct could bring joy or sorrow to others. Falconi's "buddy" was late to reveille one morning and he drew the demerit.

But this was the only black mark in an otherwise spotless six months spent at OCS. He came out number one in his class and was offered a regular Army commission. The brand-new second lieutenant happily accepted the honor and set out to begin this new phase of his career in an army he had learned to love as much as his father did.

His graduation didn't result in an immediate assignment to an active duty unit. Falconi found himself once more in school, but these were not filled with hours of poring over books. He attended jump school and earned his silver parachutists' badge; next was ranger school where he won the coveted orange-and-black tab; then he was shipped down to Panama for jungle warfare school where he garnered yet one more insignia and qualification.

Following that, he suffered another disappointment. Again, his desire to sink himself into a regular unit was thwarted. Because he held a regular army commission rather than a reserve one like his other classmates, Falconi was returned to Fort Benning to attend the Infantry school. The courses he took were designed to give him some thorough instruction in staff procedures. He came out on top here as well, but there was another thing that happened to him.

His intellectual side finally blossomed.

The theory of military science, rather than complete practical application, began to fascinate him. During his time in combat—and the later army schooling—he had begun to develop certain theories. With the exposure to Infantry school, he decided to do something about these ideas of his. He wrote several articles for the *Infantry Journal* about these thoughts—particularly on his personal analysis of the proper conduct of jungle and mountain operations involving insurgency and counterinsurgency forces.

The Army was more than a little impressed with this first lieutenant (he had been promoted) and sent him back to Panama to serve on a special committee that would develop and publish U.S. Army policy on small-unit combat operations in tropical climates. He honed his skills and tactical expertise during this time.

From there he volunteered for Special Forces— the Green Berets—and was accepted. After completing the officers' course at Fort Bragg, North Carolina, Falconi was finally assigned to a real unit for the first time since his commission. This was the Fifth Special Forces Group in the growing conflict in South Vietnam.

He earned his captaincy while working closely with ARVN units. He even helped to organize village militias to protect hamlets against the Viet Cong and North Vietnamese. Gradually, his duties expanded until he organized and led several dangerous missions that involved deep penetration into territory controlled by the communist guerrillas.

It was after a series of these operations that he was linked up with the CIA officer Clayton Andrews. Between their joint efforts, the Black Eagles had been brought into existence, and it was as the commander of that unit that Lieutenant Colonel Robert Falconi now carried on his war against the communists.

Fifteen missions were now under his belt. There had been no medals, for such accolades were not for men who serve in clandestine, near illegal units that operate in the shadowy violence of highly classified operations. It had been bloody and heartbreaking, finally working its way to a point where he now sat in a bunker far out in the Vietnamese boondocks while a heavy monsoon rain swept across the sandbagged roofs, driven by gusts of heavy winds.

Calcitra Clunis, baby!

CHAPTER 5

Major Rory Riley splashed through the mud puddles, oblivious of the driving rain that beat down on his poncho. While he struggled through the downpour, he could see the huddled inhabitants inside the bunkers. These were his Green Beret troops. They were energetic sorts who were slowly going crazy during the inactivity forced on them by the weather.

Riley, though one grade in rank lower than Lieutenant Colonel Robert Falconi, was the actual commander of Camp Nui Dep. This was due to his position as leader of the Special Forces "B" and "A" teams, as well as the native militia stationed in the fortified garrison.

Riley stepped under the canvas awning stretched over the front door of the dispensary. "Hello!" he called out, knocking on the screened portal. "Anybody home?"

Andrea Thuy, properly dressed in the fatigue uniform of a South Vietnamese Army captain, came to the screen door. "Good morning, Major," she said.

"Hi, Captain Thuy," Riley said. "My militia commander says you got a load of ailing children bedded down here in your little hospital. I just came to check on the report."

"Sure," Andrea said. "I'll let Nurse Pemberton fill you in."

"Thanks," Riley said.

He started to enter, but Andrea stopped him. "Sorry. We can't have you tracking mud in, Major. You'll have to take off your boots."

"Dang, Captain!" Riley complained in good-natured humor. "Don't rank have no privileges around here?"

"Sorry. Only sick kids," Andrea replied, smiling. "We've got to be as clean as possible here," she explained. "If you don't want to walk around in your stocking feet, I'll have Betty Lou come over."

"Call her, please. I really don't have time to get in and out of my boots. I have a complaining supply sergeant waiting for me over at my office."

Andrea did as requested. First Lieutenant Betty Lou Pemberton, also dressed in fatigues but wearing a stethoscope around her neck, made an informal report to Camp Nui Dep's commander.

"We have a virus of sorts, sir," Betty Lou said. "It's nothing serious, just a cold, but some of the children are running slight fevers. I thought it best to get them into the dispensary for a few nights of antibiotics and warm beds."

"I see," Riley said. "A good idea. Those huts they live in are drafty and damp in the monsoon. I just wanted to make sure there was nothing that could be chalked up as a medical emergency brewing here."

Jean McCorckel, Malpractice's wife, joined the other nurse. *"Chao ong, Thieu-ta* Riley," she greeted.

"Chao Ba McCorckel," Riley responded in fluent Vietnamese. *"Ba manh khong?"*

"I am fine, thank you," Jean said. "We have some bad colds here, but the little ones wil be fine soon."

"That's great," Riley said. "You three ladies are doing a wonderful job for the militiamen and their families. They really appreciate it, believe me." He winked at them. "It's taking everything in my power to keep those Green Beret guys of mine from going on sick call, too. I told 'em you ladies were here for the villagers only."

"They're nice people," Betty Lou said. "Some of the children's mothers are helping us out."

Riley peered inside and could see several of the small women sitting by the beds of their sleeping kids. "I know you're busy, so I won't take up any more of your time," Riley said. "See you later." He turned and walked back out into the rain. As he headed back for his headquarters bunker, he sighted a familiar figure trudging toward him. Riley called out, "Falconi!"

Falconi peered out from under his poncho hood. "Hi ya, Riley." He walked over to the major. "How're you doing today?"

"Pretty damned good, thanks to you and your guys," Riley said.

"Give it a break," Falconi said.

"C'mon, Falconi! I was a goddamned prisoner in

67

a wooden cage before you guys came and got me away from the Charlies," Riley said. "I'll never be able to properly thank you for that." At one time, the Green Berets had been bitter enemies with the Black Eagles. Several brawls had rolled across Nui Dep, and Archie Dobbs once smashed up Riley's jeep. But the major was no longer antagonistic toward Falconi or his men.

"You've been sending over beer every night," Falconi said. "Everybody appreciates the gesture."

During their last operation behind enemy lines, the Black Eagles had received a supplementary mission to rescue a Green Beret held prisoner by the Viet Cong. When they rescued the guy, they were surprised to find their old nemesis Major Rory Riley was the POW concerned. As far as Riley was concerned, all the old grudges and arguments melted away. His gratitude was endless.

"You Black Eagles are okay," Riley said with enthusiasm. "I don't care what General Taggart is saying about you back at SOG headquarters."

"We appreciate your support, Riley," Falconi said. "I'll pass it on to the guys."

"You bet, Falconi. See you later."

"Yeah." Falconi watched Riley splash across the compound. The lieutenant colonel continued on his own way to the dispensary. When he got there, he slipped under the awning and pulled off his shiny wet poncho. After hanging it up on hooks provided on the building's outer wall, he removed his muddy boots. When he went inside, he saw Jean McCorckel filling small paper cups with pills. Falconi nodded to her. "How're the little ones getting along?"

"Just fine, Robert," Jean said. "It is nice that all the soldiers ask about them."

"G.I.s are crazy about kids," Falconi said. "Of course, most of 'em come over here just to see you beautiful ladies."

"You are a flatterer, Robert," Jean said with a shy smile.

"Where is Andrea?" Falconi asked.

"She is back in the office," Jean said. "Andrea is much help to us. We tend the sick and she tends the paperwork. Damned *tot,* that Andrea."

"You bet," Falconi agreed. He padded to the rear of the building where a small office was located. He could hear the typewriter clacking as he approached. "Andrea?"

"Yes, Robert," she called out. "Come in."

He joined her in the office, walking around to give her a quick kiss on the lips. "I want to talk to you."

"Now that's romantic," Andrea complained.

"It's important," he said. He looked out the door and could see Betty Lou Pemberton at the far end of the ward. "What the hell's going on between Betty Lou and Archie?"

"It's commitment time, baby," Andrea said.

"What the hell does that mean?"

"What it means is that Archie is either going to make their relationship a deep and permanent one, or Betty Lou is going to split the sheets," Andrea said. *"Comprendez?"*

"Yeah!" Falconi snapped. "It's Nag-The-Guy-To-Death time."

"Lighten up," Andrea said. "Betty Lou's tour is up and she's headed back to the World. She wants

69

Archie to go with her. And there's nothing wrong in that."

"Archie is a Black Eagle," Falconi said.

"Betty Lou is not," Andrea retorted. "She wants Archie to rotate with her."

"He's an enlisted man and she's an officer," Falconi said. "The Army won't tolerate the situation."

Andrea shrugged. "They can get around that. Besides, she'll be getting out of the Army soon, so it won't make any difference."

"To each their own," Falconi said. "But right now Archie is distracted and not himself. His morale is a disaster area."

"Poor baby," Andrea said.

Falconi sighed. "It's something he'll have to work out." He smiled. "For the first time in his life, he's got another human being to take into consideration."

"You might lose Archie, Robert," Andrea pointed out.

"Yeah," Falconi agreed. "He'll be the first guy to check out of the detachment that wasn't in a body bag."

"Quite a distinction," Andrea said.

"One he might not want," Falconi said. "I may need a hand on this one."

"Let me warn you, I won't stand in love's way," Andrea said.

"Well, at least keep me informed so I can stay on top of the situation," Falconi said.

"That I can do," Andrea promised.

"Fine. I've got to get back to the bunker. See you later."

"Robert," Andrea called after him. "Leave Archie alone! Like you said so well: for the first time in his life, he has to make a serious decision that will affect not only his own future, but somebody else's, too."

"Okay, Andrea," Falconi said. "I'll let him work it out on his own. But I don't want it affecting his attitude toward his duties."

Andrea glanced out the window at the driving rain. "There won't be many duties for him anyhow in this weather."

"Lui lai!" Battalion Commander Ngoyen Li shouted over the sound of the rain. "Move that mortar back. You are too far forward."

"Yes, Comrade Battalion Commander," the mortar gunner called back. He had his crew reposition the tripod of the Soviet weapon.

Ngoyen Li turned his attention back to the sketch map he held in his hand. An umbrella, in the grasp of an eager guerrilla, kept water off the document. "This is a most precise sketch," Ngoyen Li said.

"Thank you, Comrade Battalion Commander," the young soldier said. "I climbed a tree overlooking the camp and took my time so I could do a good job."

Ngoyen Li laughed. "Did not the Yankees or their running dog militiamen see you?"

The soldier shook his head. *"Khong go,* Comrade Battalion Commander. They did not."

71

"What is your name, Comrade Soldier?"

"I am called Tai, Comrade Battalion Commander."

"I am going to have you detached from your section and assigned to me, Comrade Soldier Tai," Ngoyen Li said. "Our maneuverability will be sorely reduced during the monsoon fighting. We will have to rely heavily on our mortars and machine guns. A good mapman will be very helpful."

"I am proud to help, Comrade Battalion Commander."

"Now let us check the lay of our battery," Ngoyen Li said.

The mortar crews were busy with sights and aiming stakes as they went through the work of aligning the tubes of the shell-throwing weapons. This was done so that any azimuths called for by forward observers would be the same for every gun. It was intricate work but easily taken care of by experienced mortarmen. However, in the poor visibility of a driving rain it was twice as difficult to correctly accomplish.

Ngoyen Li, with years of experience in fighting while poorly armed in both bad weather and impossible terrain, lent a hand when he could. If a young Viet Cong needed encouragement, the old campaigner lifted his spirits with compliments and a small pep talk. On the other hand, if the guerrilla was moody or angered by the unpleasant circumstances, Ngoyen Li would be abrupt and harsh, causing the offender to be embarrassed and ashamed.

There were actually four mortar sections to see to. Each had three tubes, so that when the laying in was finally completed, a total of twelve 82-millimeter M1937 Russian heavy mortars were aligned and ready to rain flaming, slicing hell down on Nui Dep.

A rifle company arrived on the scene. Its commander, a veteran officer, reported to Ngoyen Li. "Comrade Battalion Commander, I beg to announce we are ready to take our place in the line."

Ngoyen Li, recognizing an old friend, displayed his gap-toothed grin. "Ah, Khung, faithful comrade!"

"It is good to fight with you again, Comrade Battalion Commander," Khung said. He was a tough officer, but had a sense of humor. "So we are out in the rain again, eh? I see you have an umbrella."

Ngoyen Li laughed. "It is only to keep the rain off my map when I refer to it."

"Ah, *tot!* I was afraid you were getting soft in your old age, Comrade Battalion Commander."

"Khong go! I am meaner than ever," Ngoyen Li said. "Have they explained your mission to you?"

"Only that I am to lead my men across the barbed wire after our mortar battery ceases fire," Khung said. "I presume we are to kill all the Americans and their Vienamese curs when we are inside the camp."

"That is correct, Comrade Company Commander Khung," Ngoyen Li said. He checked his watch. Every man with the rank of squad leader up was issued one. "You must move your men into position quickly. Our glorious battle starts soon."

73

"Yes, Comrade Battalion Commander." Khung turned to his men. *"Mau len!* The front line awaits us."

Ngoyen Li watched the energetic, devoted guerrillas trot past him on their way to battle. He looked over at Tai. "Tomorrow is going to be a glorious day for Chairman Ho."

"Long live Chairman Ho!" Tai exclaimed. "Death to the Americans!"

CHAPTER 6

Crump!

The sound was almost impossible to hear over the driving rain. People who lay awake in their bunkers and huts had to listen hard to make sure they'd heard correctly. Some of the garrison's younger inhabitants were unable to figure out what the persistent disturbance in the natural rhythm of the monsoon night was.

Crump!

But the ears of Nui Deps' numerous combat veterans could easily recognize the noise: mortar fire! And they knew of the unspeakable hell that would soon follow.

Crump!

The very experienced of the camp's inhabitants could identify what particular type of weapon was blasting away—Soviet M1937 heavy mortars. Those killing machines could be fired at a rate of fifteen to twenty-five times per minute, depending on the proficiency and experience of the crew. With a range of over three thousand meters, their high-explosive shells reached long and fell accurately.

Crump! Crump! Crump!

The enemy fired a total of forty-eight times before the first shells fell on the camp.

The Black Eagle bunker shook with the force of the concussion from the detonating mortar rounds. The sleeping men's minds leaped to full wakefulness when the howling splatters of wicked shrapnel slapped the sandbags, making hundreds of popping sounds.

"To your positions!" Sergeant Major Top Gordon shouted above the roaring din. "They'll be dropping this shit on us for a while, so you got time to get your boots and clothes on. Move it! We ain't gonna spend the whole frigging night taking this shit without doing nothing about it. Move it!"

The men complied, instinctively ducking as particularly close explosions rocked their shelter. Within a matter of a few short minutes, all were fully dressed with M16s and full bandoleers of ammunition slung over their shoulders. They crouched beneath their individual firing slits, waiting for the unexpected salvos to evolve into a full-blown battle.

Two of the men, however, had more than just their personal safety in mind. Archie Dobbs and Malpractice McCorckel were worried about their two women over at the dispensary. They were also concerned about Andrea Thuy who, as a companion-at-arms, also rated their attention. The pair of Black Eagles huddled together as the pounding of the heavy weapons continued.

Archie leaned close to Malpractice's ear. "We

gotta get them women back here."

Malpractice nodded his head in agreement, but was more pragmatic. "They got a shelter over at the dispensary, so they'll get them kids down into it."

"I suppose," Archie said. "And they won't leave 'em alone there neither."

"They sure as hell won't," Malpractice agreed. "So we won't be able to talk 'em into coming back here with us."

Archie held up his M16 rifle. "Maybe not. So that means they can use a couple o' hardcases like us with weapons. If the Charlies bust through the perimeter, they'll be all over that dispensary like stink on shit."

"You're right," Malpractice said. He glanced over at Top Gordon who was giving his full attention to the far side of the bunker. "Here's our chance. C'mon, Archie. Let's go!"

"I'm with you," Archie said.

The two Black Eagles eased toward the bunker door. They hesitated only after a loud series of detonations marched across the top of the bunker. When the last of the shells slammed into the soft ground outside, they made their move.

Archie led the way up the bunker steps. He charged through the poncho covering over the doorway with Malpractice right behind him. They hadn't taken more than a dozen running steps when the thundering hell of incoming rounds engulfed the garrison once more. They made a valiant effort to move forward, but it was impossible. The mortar barrage had every area of the camp well covered. Archie and Malpractice retreated back to the bunker and dove down into the safety of its interior.

Top Gordon, who had caught a glimpse of them as they disappeared up the steps, was livid with rage. "Who told you two stupid sonofabitches you could leave?"

A particularly loud explosion rocked the place, making heavy clouds of dust filter down from the ceiling.

"We're out to look after our women," Archie answered defiantly. "They're all by their lonesome with them kids in the shelter."

"Get back to your posts," Top said. "I'll deal with you two later. Too bad they outlawed flogging in the American armed forces."

"Yeah? Well, I bet you was in the Army when the law was passed," Archie said in sullen anger.

Top's bellowing reply was lost in another blasting sound of incoming shells.

Falconi pushed his way through the crowded bunker. "You two tend to your duties, goddamnit!"

"We're real concerned about the girls, sir," Archie protested.

"Jesus! Don't you think I'm worried sick about Andrea?"

"Yes, sir," Malpractice said, shamefaced.

"We're sorry," Archie said weakly.

Falconi's voice could no longer be heard as the mortar fire increased, but the rage in his expression was enough to subdue any further rebellious thoughts by Archie and Malpractice.

The lucky children whose mothers had accompanied them to the hospital huddled in terror. But they at least had the advantage of being comforted by the feeling of familiar hugs and the sound of their moms' loving voices.

The others clung to Andrea, Betty Lou, and Jean. The three women did their best to calm the terrified youngsters. But the plaintive cries of *"Ma toi!"* could be heard between the explosions.

"Stay as calm as you can," Andrea urged her companions.

Jean McCorckel had been through war before, but Betty Lou's experience had only been the aftermath of the fighting and violence when she helped patch up the wounded and maimed survivors. The American nurse licked her dry lips and displayed a weak smile. "I promise to try. But I'm not sure I can do it, Andrea."

Andrea continued to act calm. "You must, dear," she said in a soothing voice. "The children will panic if we act the least bit frightened."

Betty Lou nodded, hugging two of the children close to her.

There was a momentary break in the blasts. Jean took advantage of the brief calm. She leaned close to the children, saying, *"Durng so*—don't be afraid."

Betty Lou picked up the short phrase in Vietnamese. *"Durng so,"* she repeated softly. *"Durng so."*

Another string of mortar shells moved across the camp, making the ground shake and roll with the force of fiery thunder. The children screamed in terror as the nurses continued to do their best to comfort them.

"Durng so. Durng so."

* * *

Up on the Viet Cong front line, Company Commander Khung's men lay flat, hugging the wet ground as the shells fired by their comrades flew past overhead and slammed down onto the objective a hundred meters to the front.

Except for not being affected by the shrapnel, the awful bombardment's effect was tough on them, too. The noise and concussion pounded their eardrums, causing many of the guerrillas to bleed from their ears. But they found consolation in the fact that the shells were pounding the hell out of the positions they would shortly be charging against. Each series of crashes that heralded another barrage were sounds of solace to the Viet Cong riflemen.

But suddenly there was silence.

Company Commander Khung did not waste a precious moment. He blew his whistle. *"Tien len! Advance!"* he commanded.

His company of fighters, the leading unit in the assault, leaped to their feet and rushed forward through the rain. The target looked eerie even to the veterans as they stormed through the blasted, useless barbed wire on Nui Dep's ruined defensive perimeter.

Small fires of explosive-caused rubble cast dancing light that sparkled off the thickly falling drops of rain. Ruined bunker roofs, now nothing but split sandbags and twisted sheet iron, glistened under the heavy showers. Shell holes, blasted by the previous mortar barrage, had already filled with muddy water. Except for the detonated man-made structures, it appeared almost as a scene from another world.

When the first ranks of Viet Cong reached the

perimeter, they met no resistance. For a few seconds, the young guerrillas thought that all the camp's personnel had been killed.

Then Major Rory Riley's Special Forces machine gunners went into action.

Crisscrossing streaks of .50 and .30 caliber slugs swept across the first row of Charlies, blowing them down in unresisting heaps. Their comrades behind picked up the pace and hurried forward. More numerous and formed closer, they were able to penetrate farther into the camp. But they met the same fate.

Company Commander Khung knew that the success of this spearhead movement depended on gaining a distinct advantage within the first few minutes of the attack. Furious at the thought of being thrown back, he ordered more sections forward until his entire unit was charging into the murderous fire of Riley's men.

Out in the jungle, squatting by the radio operator in his impromptu command post, Battalion Commander Ngoyen Li listened to the broadcast of his forward observer. The young map-maker Tai had been given the privilege of this duty. It was an honor to be entrusted with such responsibility, because the Viet Cong did not have a plethora of communications equipment. There were only two radios in his entire battalion. Thus, Tai's appointment to use one of the valuable instruments showed the huge amount of trust that Ngoyen Li had in him.

The battalion commander had grown worried when Tai at the front reported that Khung's company had faltered after an initial penetration. Ngoyen Li ordered another company in to reinforce the effort, but Tai's voice, distorted by the Chinese-made radio, brought no encouraging news.

"Comrade Battalion Commander," Tai said over the air. "The comrades have been stopped before entering the main area of the camp."

Ngoyen Li impatiently grabbed the microphone from the nervous radio operator with him. "Comrade Forward Observer," Ngoyen Li said. "Call me back if they move forward or if they fall back."

Ten minutes passed while the rate of machine-gun fire built up to a point that it drowned out the sound of the AK47s.

Tai came back on the air. "Comrade Battalion Commander, the comrades are returning to the jungle. They leave many dead and wounded behind."

Ngoyen Li shouted over at his mortar battery commander, "Begin firing again."

The officer immediately issued the necessary orders. Within short seconds, the 62-millimeter shells were being dropped down the tubes. They hit the firing pins at the base, exploding the plastic charges that fired them back into the correct trajectories to fall onto Camp Nui Dep.

Up at the front, the first shells even fell among the fleeing Viet Cong. Mortar rounds have no minds or souls. They care nothing about who is killed by their deadly shrapnel. This ammunition, manufactured in Communist China, blew the unfortunate Red guerrillas to bloody hunks of dead humanity with detonating, killing efficiency.

*   *   *

The action down at the Black Eagles' side of camp had been hot and heavy, too. A two-pronged attack had hit their sector, but Falconi's cool command style had resulted in devastating defense fire that kept the Viet Cong at bay.

For a few brief seconds it appeared as if the detachment would be able to mount an effective counterattack, but the renewal of incoming mortar rounds forced them back into their bunker. Now, in spite of the anxiety they felt for the women, Archie and Malpractice had made no efforts to temporarily go AWOL. The few terse words from Falconi had been enough to put them on the straight and narrow. But Sergeant Major Top Gordon kept a sharp eye on the two just in case.

The Black Eagles crouched in the bunker enduring the second barrage. When that one finally lifted, the detachment manned their firing slits. They knew the Viet Cong would be trying another assault on their position. Falconi, however, did not plan to remain in a defensive posture for long. He fully meant to follow their motto of *Calcitra Clunis*— Kick Ass!

The lieutenant colonel waited for their return fire to slow down the VC infantry attack. Gunnar Olson and Paulo Garcia had been appointed automatic riflemen. On command, they cut loose with long sprays of full-auto fire that wiped out the forward echelon of the Viet Cong.

"Let's go!" Falconi ordered. "As skirmishers!"

The detachment raced up the steps and out the back of the bunker. Half went to the right, and half to the left, both teams going around to the front.

When they emerged on the other side, they formed up and moved forward. By then Gunnar and Paulo had joined them, and the Black Eagles moved forward throwing out intertwining volleys of rapid fire

The VC resistance stiffened. For a full five minutes the situation was touch and go for both sides. Then the superior fire-power and command direction of the Black Eagles came to the fore, and the Red guerrillas melted away in front of them. Cheering, the detachment rushed forward to pursue the now-fleeing Charlies into the jungle.

Then the battle from the other side of the camp rolled in on them.

Major Rory Riley, with his combined command of Green Berets and native militia, had been especially hard hit. They fought valiantly, but overwhelming numbers of enemy troops pressured them into a retreat. The militiamen's families fled behind the fighting. The situation quickly deteriorated when these frightened noncombatants finally bumped into Falconi and his Black Eagles. Within moments, the remainder of the camp's defenders were also pressed in on them.

Now, under the screaming tracers of incoming fire, the garrison had been turned into a milling, helpless mob.

The Viet Cong radio operator called out happily to his leader, "Comrade Battalion Commander! The comrade forward observer calls for you!"

Ngoyen Li rushed over to the crude commo center

and grabbed the microphone. "Yes, Comrade Forward Observer?"

"Comrade Battalion Commander, the enemy has been pushed back into one corner of the camp. They are now helpless before our comrades."

Ngoyen Li didn't bother to answer. He tossed the mike back, and turned to spring through the dripping jungle. His objective wasn't far away. Khung's company, exhausted from bearing the brunt of the fighting, squatted in rest.

Ngoyen Li found their commander and pulled him to his feet, glaring at him. "Comrade! Victory is now ours! But you must bring your men to one more effort. I fear the other comrade company commanders do not have the drive and ability to bring this battle to a glorious end."

Khung needed no further urging. He turned away, bellowing orders. Within a few short moments, his company—at least what was left of it after the mauling they took—was up and moving. Khung wanted to deliver a final blow to the stubborn defenders who had decimated his command.

Both Lieutenant Colonel Robert Falconi and Major Rory Riley worked like madmen to bring some order to the chaos that Camp Nui Dep had sunk into.

Black Eagles and Green Berets bodily pulled women and children from the masses of native militia, herding them into a safe area between the detachment bunker and a fortified observation post. Once this was done, the panic-stricken husbands

85

and fathers of these noncombatants were pummeled and pushed into a semblance of combat formations. Gradually, as the Americans' voices began to calm them, these indigenous fighters responded to the instructions.

Suddenly the enemy firing stepped up; then another attack was launched. The Viet Cong streamed across the camp and pushed inward toward the small area still held by the defenders.

"Ban! Ban! Fire!" Falconi ordered.

The militiamen, interspersed with Americans, suddenly found their courage once again. Well-armed and equipped, they responded properly for the first time since the surprise assault had been launched against the camp. Sparkling tracers intertwined as they flew like countless burning hornets into the close-packed masses of Charlies.

The Viet Cong NCOs and officers urged their men to greater effort. The Reds crammed forward over the falling bodies of their comrades. But the momentum of their mass charge slowly faltered, then came to a halt.

The coup de grâce was administered by Sergeant Gunnar Olson. He had taken a quick break to fetch his Soviet RPK light machine gun from the Black Eagle bunker. The Minnesotan had acquired the effective weapon during the unit's previous mission. Working with 75-round drum magazines, Gunnar hosed a tremendous amount of support fire to intermingle with the flying bullets of the Americans and Vietnamese militia.

It was more than the Charlies could stand.

Company Commander Khung screamed in rage,

but his men ignored him. They broke and fled back into the soaking jungle, abandoning weapons, gear, dead, and wounded in their hysterical desire to escape the blazing hell thrown at them.

The empty space between the Nui Dep men and the attackers was quickly filled by Falconi and his Black Eagles. They rushed forward to deliver more death to the routed Reds.

Now Archie Dobbs and Malpractice McCorckel broke off from the main body. They sprinted and leaped over and through the rubble of the blasted camp. The pair found the dispensary blown away. It was nothing but a tangle of pulverized, splintered wood.

Archie turned toward the shelter and ran to the entrance. "Betty Lou! Betty Lou!" he yelled out. "Andrea! Jean!" He disappeared down the steps, then quickly reappeared.

Malpractice, streaked with raindrops that cut through the dirt on his face, grimaced. "What'd you find?"

"Nothing," Archie said. "They're all gone, Malpractice. I swear to God! The goddamned Charlies have kidnapped 'em!"

CHAPTER 7

The sting of defeat smarted right down to the core of Battalion Commander Ngoyen Li's psyche. His very soul boiled with shame and rage.

The Viet Cong officer's bold plan, so difficult to put into operation because of the opposition from high-ranking staff officers and their Russian advisers, had been ripped apart. The unique idea of carrying on a surprise attack in the depth of the monsoon had seemed almost insane. But Ngoyen Li energetically pointed out that it would succeed because such action would be completely unexpected. Long days of argument had finally paid off. The Russians had nodded a silent agreement, giving their little brothers in the North Vietnamese Army a strong hint to go along with the idea. The senior NVA officer picked up the operations plan and signed it. Ngoyen Li's scheme for a surprise attack had finally been approved.

Unfortunately, the mission had gone from a carefully plotted military combat activity to a tactical joke. And Ngoyen Li had recognized that a certain unit within Camp Nui Dep's defenses had done the most damage.

Ngoyen Li, with his loyal soldier Tai at his heels, plodded through the rain-swept forest. In his anger, he had not waited to see the surviving front line troops return from the botched assault. The VC officer had moved off ahead of them, not wanting to look at the defeated guerrillas. Now he didn't even notice the wet and cold as he moved along with the column of men. His mind seethed as he tried to figure out not only what had gone wrong, but why.

His black reveries were finally interrupted by the radio operator who trailed him by a short distance. "Comrade Battalion Commander, there is a broadcast from Comrade Company Commander Khung."

Ngoyen Li turned back and joined the commo man. He spoke into the mike. *"A-lo,"* he answered.

"Commander," Khung said. "I have been trying to find you in the column."

Ngoyen Li was not in a good mood. "So? You can speak to me now, Khung." He had been particularly disappointed in Khung's performance.

"Commander, we have prisoners," Khung said.

"Co? I am surprised. They must have been manning an outpost. At any rate, we cannot transport POWs. Shoot them, quickly!"

"But, Commander! These are special. We have children of villagers and their mothers, and—"

Ngoyen Li interrupted. "Our comrade commissary officer cannot even fill small bellies, Khung. Execute the prisoners without further delay."

"Commander, listen to me! We have nurses, too.

90

One is a Vietnamese civilian, one is in the South Vietnamese Army, and the other is in the American Army."

Ngoyen Li was stunned. For a moment he could not speak. "Bring them forward to me for immediate questioning," he finally said.

"What about the other women and children?" Khung asked. "Shall I have the soldiers dispatch them?"

"Khong co—no! All these prisoners may prove valuable," Ngoyen Li said. Now that his temper was simmering down a bit, Ngoyen Li began to think in a clearer manner. "We will use the village women as joy girls. It will serve them right for being married to men of the native militia. But right now the most important thing is to examine the nurses."

"Yes, Comrade Battalion Commander," Khung said. "I shall report to you immediately."

Lieutenant Colonel Robert Falconi's Black Eagles wasted no time in pursuing the fleeing Viet Cong. Always ready for instant action, they had only to draw fresh ammo loads and rations from Rory Riley's S4 bunker. Then, fully equipped for a long session of jungle fighting, they'd left the meager warmth and comfort offered by the smashed bunkers of Camp Nui Dep to track down the captors of the women and children.

The mission was doubly important because the reputation and reliability of the combination American-South Vietnamese self-defense program was at stake. If the Viet Cong showed they could pull

91

off a surprise attack and kidnap the women and children of militiamen enrolled in the project, they would score a great moral and physical victory which would bring mutual efforts at cooperation with the Saigon and American governments crashing to a dismal defeat.

As the Black Eagles followed their scout Archie Dobbs through the wet-slicked, dripping vegetation of the monsoon jungle, Falconi took time to glance over his special troops.

And he liked what he saw.

There was First Lieutenant Ray Swift Elk. This full-blooded Sioux Indian was lean and muscular. His copper-colored skin, hawkish nose, and high cheekbones gave him the appearance of the classic prairie warrior. The great artists of the American West, Remington and Russell, could have used him as the perfect model in their portrayals of the noble Red Man. But beneath his outward appearance, Ray Swift Elk had one hell of an army service record. As a matter of fact, there were still dark spots on his fatigues where he'd removed his master sergeant chevrons after his battlefield commission. Brand-new cloth insignia of an infantry lieutenant were sewn on his collars.

Twelve years of service in Special Forces had made Swift Elk particularly well qualified to be the detachment executive officer. This particular position was important because, in reality, he was Falconi's second in command.

In spite of his skills and education in modern soldiering, Swift Elk still considered his ancestral past an important part of his life, and he practiced

Indian customs when and where able. Part of his tribe's history included some vicious combat against the Black troopers of the U.S. Cavalry's 9th and 10th Cavalry regiments of the racially segregated army of the nineteenth century. The Sioux warriors had nicknamed the black men they fought "Buffalo Soldiers." This was because of their hair which, to the Indians, was like the thick manes on the buffalo. The appellation was a sincere compliment because these native Americans venerated the bison. Ray Swift Elk called Calvin Culpepper, the black guy in the detachment, "Buffalo Soldier," and he did so with the same respect his ancestors demonstrated toward Uncle Sam's black horse troopers during the violent Plains wars.

The next man in the Black Eagle chain of command was Sergeant Major Top Gordon. As the senior noncommissioned officer of the Black Eagles, he was tasked with several administrative and command responsibilities. Besides having to take any issued operations plans and use them to form the basic operations orders for the missions, he was also responsible for maintaining discipline and efficiency within the unit.

Top was a husky man, his jet-black hair thinning perceptibly, looking even more sparse because of the strict G.I. haircut he wore. His entrance into the Black Eagles had been less than satisfactory. After seventeen years spent in the Army's elite spit-and-polish airborne infantry units, he had brought in an attitude that did not fit well with the diverse individuals in Falconi's command. Gordon's zeal to follow army regulations to the letter had cost him a marriage when his wife, fed up with having a husband who thought more of the Army than her, filed for divorce and took their kids back to the old hometown in upstate New York. Despite that heartbreaking experience, he hadn't let up a bit. To make the situation for him even more difficult during his first days in the Black Eagles, he had taken the place of a popular detachment sergeant who was killed in action on the Song Bo River. This noncom, called "Top" by the men, was an old Special Forces man who knew how to handle the type of soldier who volunteered for unconventional units. Any new top sergeant would have been resented no matter what type of man he was.

Gordon's premier appearance in his new assignment brought him into quick conflict with the Black Eagle personnel. Within only hours, the situation had gotten so far out of hand that Falconi began to seriously consider relieving the sergeant and seeing to his transfer back to a regular airborne unit.

But during Operation Laos Nightmare, Gordon's bravery under fire earned him the grudging respect of the lower-ranking Black Eagles. Finally, when he fully realized the problems he had created for himself, he changed his methods of leadership. Gordon backed off doing things by the book and found he could still maintain good discipline and efficiency while getting rid of the chicken-shit aspects of army life. It was most apparent he had been accepted by the men when they bestowed the nickname "Top" on him.

He had truly become the "top sergeant" then. But his natural gruffness and short temper remained the same. Nothing could change those characteristics.

The detachment medic, Sergeant First Class Malcomb "Malpractice" McCorckel, an original member of the unit, was always right on Top Gordon's heels. An inch under six feet in height, Malpractice had been in the Army for twelve years. He had a friendly face and spoke softly as he pursued his duties in seeing after the illnesses and hurts of his buddies. He nagged and needled each and every one of them in order to keep that wild bunch healthy. They bitched back at him, but not angrily, because each Black Eagle appreciated the medical sergeant's concern. They all knew that nothing devised by puny man—not even mortar fire or grenades—could keep Malpractice from reaching a wounded detachment member and pulling him back to safety. Malpractice was unique in the unit for another reason, too. He was the only married man under Falconi's command.

The detachment's slowest, easiest-going guy, Petty Officer Blue Richards was a fully qualified Navy Seal. Besides his fighting skills, his special claim to fame was his uncanny tree-climbing abilities. When it was necessary to go high to get a good look around, Blue could be counted on to shinny up even the tallest trees. A red-haired Alabamian with a gawky, good-natured grin common to good ol' country boys, Blue had been named after his "daddy's favorite huntin' dawg." An expert in demolitions either on land or underwater, Blue considered himself honored for his father to have given him that dog's name.

Then there was Marine Staff Sergeant Paulo

Garcia. Under the new reorganization of the detachment that was necessary after suffering such heavy casualties, Paulo performed both the communications and intelligence work for the Black Eagles. Of Portuguese descent, this former tuna fisherman from San Diego, California, had joined the Marines at the relatively late age of twenty-one after deciding to look for a bit of adventure. There was always Marine Corps activity to see around his hometown, and he decided that fighting group offered him exactly what he was looking for. Ten years of service and plenty of combat action in the Demilitarized Zone and Khe Sanh made him more than qualified for the Black Eagles.

Sergeant First Class Calvin Culpepper was a tall, brawny black man who had entered the Army off a poor Georgia farm his family had worked as sharecroppers. Although once a team leader in the detachment, the new setup got him back to his usual job of handling all the senior demolition chores. His favorite tool in that line of work was C4 plastic explosive. It was said he could set off a charge under a silver dollar and get back ninety-nine cents change. Resourceful, intelligent, and combatwise, Calvin, called the "Buffalo Soldier" by Lieutenant Ray Swift Elk, pulled his weight—and then a bit more—in the dangerous undertakings of the Black Eagles.

The newest man was Army Sergeant Gunnar Olson, who had officially taken part in one Black Eagle mission before his actual assignment to the detachment. This had been during the operation on the Song Cai River when he'd been a gunner—

appropriately called Gunnar the Gunner—on a helicopter gunship that flew fire support operations for Falconi and his men. Gunnar was so impressed with the detachment that he immediately put in for a transfer to the unit. Falconi quickly approved the paperwork and hired Gunnar the Gunner on as the unit's heavy weapons man. Now armed with an M70 grenade launcher and a .45 caliber automatic pistol, Gunnar, of Norwegian descent from Minnesota, looked forward to continued service with the detachment, despite the mauling they'd taken on their last mission.

The man with the most perilous job in the detachment was PFC Archie Dobbs, and no other unit in the Army had a man quite like him. Formerly a brawling, beer-swilling womanizer, Archie had been a one-man public scandal and disaster area in garrison or in town. But that was before he'd found his new love, Army nurse Betty Lou Pemberton. Now his wild ways had tamed down quite a bit. But, out of control or not, once Archie was out in the field as point man and scout. In that job he went into the most dangerous areas first.

That was his trade: to see what—or who—was there. Reputed to be the best compass man in the United States Army, his seven years of service were fraught with stints in the stockade and dozens of "busts" to lower rank. Fond of women and booze, Archie's claim to fame—and the object of genuine respect from the other men—was that he had saved their asses on more than one occasion by guiding them safely through throngs of enemy troops behind the lines. Like the cat who always landed on his feet, Archie could be dropped into the middle of any geographic hell and find his way out. His sense of direction was flawless and had made him the Man of the Hour on several Black Eagle missions during dangerous exfiltration operations when everything had gone completely and totally to hell.

All those individuals made up the detachment who used *Calcitra Clunis* as its motto. Lieutenant Colonel Robert Falconi and the Black Eagles didn't like anything—or anyone—taken away from them. Furious and vengeful, they had donned their ponchos and picked up their M16s to begin a hell trek through the monsoon-drenched jungle to bring the pitiful victims back to their families. And, for three of the men, there was the double duty: of rescuing the women they loved.

The three women, shivering with cold, stood before Ngoyen Li. He studied each individually, noting they were soaked to the skin, yet more concerned for the native children than for themselves.

Andrea Thuy spoke up. "Where have you taken the other women who were with us?"

"That is not your concern, Nurse," Ngoyen Li said.

"But they were helping to care for the children," Jean interjected. "Their own little ones are still with us."

"I care nothing about the bastard offspring of running dog militiamen," Ngoyen Li said. "Do not

98

trouble me by whining for mercy to be shown those nits."

"Surely you cannot let these infants suffer so much," Betty Lou said, joining in the conversation. "These children cannot travel through this rain."

Ngoyen Li said nothing, merely regarding the woman through half-closed eyes.

"All of them were in the dispensary with ailments," Andrea said. "If they remain in this wet weather, many will get sicker and may even die."

Ngoyen Li ignored her words. "You are a Vietnamese, *khong co?* Yet you have a special look about you."

Andrea had to be careful. She knew that the North Vietnamese not only had a dossier on her, but had also offered a reward for her capture alive. She had been a prisoner of the communists several times in her life. The young Eurasian woman knew what would be in store if her true identity were discovered. She could not even reveal the French in her ancestry.

"I am an Army nurse," Andrea said. "That is all."

"You interest me," Ngoyen Li said. He turned his attention to Jean. He perceived a civilian nurse who did not seem too remarkable. The Viet Cong officer swung his gaze to Betty Lou. Here was a special problem. Although an American, she would have no useful military information. Yet the situation was so unusual that he would have to report her to his superiors. Perhaps the woman would prove a propaganda value if the right comrades could exploit her.

Betty Lou, frightened out of her wits, continued to speak up nevertheless. "I demand our release," she stated as firmly. "We are not soldiers or fighters. Only women and children. And you must let the mothers return. Please! I am begging you!"

Ngoyen Li ignored her plea. Instead, he looked back at Andrea Thuy. "I have a special interest in you."

Andrea, so full of hate she could barely control herself, gritted her teeth and remained silent.

CHAPTER 8

Andrea Thuy was, most assuredly, a commissioned officer in the South Vietnamese army. She was a beautiful Eurasian woman in her mid-twenties. Five feet six inches tall, she was svelte and trim, yet had large breasts and shapely hips and thighs that rounded out even her field uniforms with a provocative shape.

Andrea was born in a village west of Hanoi in the late 1940s. Her father, Dr. Gaston Roget, was a lay missionary physician of the Catholic Church. Deeply devoted to his native patients, the man served a large area of northern French Indochina in a dedicated, unselfish manner. The MD did not stint a bit in the giving of himself and his professional talents.

He met Andrea's mother just after the young Vietnamese woman had completed her nurse's training in Hanoi. Despite the differences in their races and ages—the doctor by then was forty-eight years old—the two fell in love and were married.

This blending of East and West produced a most beautiful child, young Andrea Roget.

Andrea's life was one of happiness. The village where she lived was devoted to *Bac-Si* Gaston, as they called her father, and this respect was passed on to the man's wife and child. When the first hint of a communist uprising brushed across the land, the good people of this hamlet rejected it out of hand. The propaganda the Reds vomited out did not fit when applied to the case of the gentle French doctor who devoted his time to looking after them. Besides, in that remote rural area, the colonial government was a faraway, unknown thing they never saw or heard from. It seemed to the villagers that it was unimportant who governed Indochina, as long as the politicians left them in peace.

Despite these reasons, the fanatical communist movement could not ignore even this subtle repudiation of their ideals. Therefore, the local Red guerrilla unit made a call on the people who would not follow the line of political philosophy they taught. To make the matter even more insidious, these agents of Soviet imperialism had hidden the true aim of their organization within the wrappings of a so-called independence movement. Many freedom-loving Indochinese fervently wanted the French out of their country so they could enjoy the fruits of self-government. They were among the first to fall for the trickery of the communist revolution.

When the Red Viet Minh came to the village, they had no intentions of devoting the visit to pacification or even winning the hearts and minds of the populace. They had come to make examples of

102

areas of the population that rejected them.

They had come to kill and destroy.

Little Andrea Roget was only three years old at the time, but she always remembered the rapine and slaughter the Red soldiers inflicted on the innocent people. Disturbing dreams and nightmares would bring back the horrible incident even into her adulthood, and the girl would recall the day with horror and revulsion.

The first people to die were Docteur and Madame Roget. Of all examples to be made, this was the most important for the murderers. The unfortunate couple was shot down before their infant daughter's eyes. The little girl could barely comprehend what had happened to her parents. Then the slaughter was turned on the village men. Executed in groups, the piles of dead grew around the huts.

Then it was the women's turn for their specific lesson in Viet Minh mercy and justice.

Hours of rape and torment went on before the females were herded together in one large group. The Soviet burp guns chattered like squawking birds of death as swarms of steel-jacketed 7.63 millimeter slugs slammed into living flesh.

Afterward, the village was burned while the wounded who had survived the first fusillades were flung screaming into the flames. When they tried to climb out of the inferno, they met the bayonets of the "liberators" of Indochina.

Finally, after this last outrage, the communist soldiery marched off singing the songs of their revolution.

It was several hours after the carnage that the

French colonial paratroopers showed up. They had received word of the crime from a young man who lived in a nearby village. He had come to see Dr. Roget regarding treatment for an ulcerated leg. After the youth had heard the shooting while approaching the hamlet, he'd left the main trail and approached in the cover offered by the jungle. Peering through the dense foliage, the young Indochinese perceived the horror. Hoping to save as many as he could, or at least get the Red gangsters captured, he limped painfully on his bad leg fifty kilometers to the nearest military post where a company of French colonial paras were garrisoned.

The paratroopers, when they arrived, were shocked. These combat veterans had seen atrocities before. They had endured having their own people taken hostage to be executed by the Gestapo during the recent war in Europe. But even the savagery of the massacre of this inconsequential little village was of such magnitude they could scarcely believe their eyes.

The commanding officer looked around at the devastation and shook his head. *"Mon Dieu! Le SS peut prendre une leçon des cettes bêtes*—the SS could take a lesson from these beasts!"

The French colonial paras searched through the smoking ruins, pulling out the charred corpses for decent burial. One grizzled trooper, his face covered with three days' growth of beard, stumbled across little Andrea who had miraculously been overlooked during the murderous binge of the Viet Minh. He knelt down beside her, his tenderest feelings brought to the surface by the sight of the pathetic, beautiful child. He gently stroked her cheek, then took her in his brawny arms and stood up.

"Oh, *pauvre enfante*," he cooed at her. "We will take you away from all this *horreur*." The paratrooper carried the little girl through the ravaged village to the road where a convoy of second-hand U.S. Army trucks waited. These vehicles, barely usable, were kept running through the desperate inventiveness of mechanics who had only the barest essentials in the way of tools and parts. But, for the French who fought this thankless war, that was only par for the course.

Little Andrea sat in the lap of the commanding officer during the tedious trip into Hanoi. The column had to halt periodically to check the road ahead for mines. There was also an ambush by the Viet Minh. While the short but fierce battle was fought, the child was protected by being hidden in a ditch until the attackers broke off the fight and sneaked away.

Upon arriving in Hanoi, the paras followed the usual procedure for war orphans and turned the girl over to a Catholic orphanage. This institution, run by the *Soeurs de la Charité*—the Sisters of Charity —did their best to check out Andrea's background. But all the records in the home village had been destroyed, and the child could say only her first name. She hadn't quite learned her last name, so all that could be garnered from her baby talk was the name "Andrea." She had inherited most of her looks from her mother; hence, she was decidedly Oriental in appearance. The nuns did not know the girl had French blood. Thus Andrea Roget was given a

Vietnamese name and became listed officially as Andrea Thuy.

Her remaining childhood at the orphanage was happy. The horrible memories receded back into her subconscious, and she concentrated on her new life. Andrea grew tall and beautiful, getting an excellent education and also learning responsibility and leadership. Parentless children were constantly showing up at the orphanage. When she reached her teens, Andrea did her part in taking care of them. This important task was expanded from the normal care and feeding of the children to teaching school. Andrea had been chosen for this extra responsibility because she was a brilliant student. The nuns, even then, were working on plans to send her to France where she would undoubtedly earn a university degree.

But Dien Bien Phu fell in 1954.

Once again, the war had touched her life with insidious cruelty. The orphanage in Hanoi had to be closed when that city became part of the newly created nation of communist North Vietnam. The gentle *Soeurs de la Charité* took their charges and moved south to organize a new orphanage in Attopeu, Laos.

Then the Pathet Lao came.

These zealots made the Viet Minh look like Sunday school teachers. Wild, fanatical, and uncivilized, these devotees of Marxism knew no limits in their war-making. Capable of unspeakable cruelty and displaying incredible savagery and stupidity, they were so terrible that they won not one convert in any of the areas they conquered.

106

Andrea was fifteen years old when the orphanage was raided. This time there was no chance for her to be overlooked or considered too inconsequential for torment. She, like all the older girls and nuns, was ravished countless times in the screaming orgy. When the rapine finally ended, the Pathet Lao set the mission's buildings on fire. But this wasn't the end of their "fun."

The nuns, because they were Europeans, were murdered. Naked, raped, and shamed, the pitiable women were flung alive into the flames. This same outrage, committed by the Viet Minh in her old village, awakened the memory of the terrible event for Andrea. She went into shock as the murder of the nuns continued.

Some screamed, but most prayed as they endured their horrible deaths. Andrea, whose Oriental features still overshadowed her French ancestry, was thought just to be another native orphan.

She endured one more round of raping with the other girls, then the Pathet Lao, having scored another victory for communism, gathered up their gear and loot to march away to the next site in their campaign of Marxist expansionism.

Andrea gathered the surviving children around her. With the nuns now gone, she was the leader of their pathetic group. Instinct told her to move south. To the north were the Red marauders and their homeland. Whatever lay in the opposite direction had to be better. She could barely remember the gruff kindness of the French paratroopers, but she did recall they went south. Andrea didn't know if these same men would be there or not, but it was worth the effort to find out.

The journey she took the other children on was long and arduous. Short of food, the little column moved south through the jungle, eating wild fruit and other vegetation. For two weeks Andrea tended her flock, sometimes carrying a little one until her arms ached with the effort. She comforted them and soothed their fears as best she could. She kept up their hope by telling them of the kind people who awaited them at the end of the long trail.

Two weeks after leaving the orphanage, Andrea sighted a patrol of soldiers. Her first reaction was of fear and alarm, but the situation of the children by then was so desperate that she had to take a chance and contact the troops. After making sure the children had concealed themselves in the dense foliage, Andrea approached the soldiers. If they were going to rape her, she figured, they would have their fun but never know the orphans were concealed nearby. Timidly, the young girl moved out onto the trail in front of them. With her lips trembling, she bowed and spoke softly.

"Chao ong."

The lead soldier, startled by her unexpected appearance, almost shot her. He relaxed a bit as he directed his friends to watch the surrounding jungle in case this was part of a diabolical Viet Cong trick. He smiled aback at the girl. *"Chao co.* What can I do for you?"

Andrea swallowed nervously but felt better when she noted there was no red star insignia on his uniform. Then she launched into a spiel about the nuns, the orphanage—everything. When the other soldiers approached and quite obviously meant her no harm, she breathed a quiet prayer of thanks under her breath.

She and the children were safe at last.

These troops, who were from the South Vietnamese Army, took the little refugees back to their detachment commander. This young lieutenant followed standard practice for such situations and made arrangements to transport Andrea and her charges farther back to higher headquarters for interrogation and eventual relocation in a safe area.

Andrea was given a thorough interview with a South Vietnamese intelligence officer. He was pleased to learn that the girl was not only well acquainted with areas now under occupation by communist troops but was also fluent in the Vietnamese, Laotian, and French languages. He passed this information on to other members of his headquarters staff for discussion as to Andrea's potential as an agent. After a lengthy conference among themselves, it was agreed to keep her in the garrison when they sent the other orphans to Saigon.

Andrea waited there while a complete background investigation was conducted into her past life. They delved so deeply into the information available on her that each item of intelligence seemed to lead to another until they discovered the truth that she didn't even know. She was a Eurasian, and her father a Frenchman—Monsieur le Docteur Gaston Roget.

This led to the girl being taken to an even higher ranking officer for her final phase of questioning. He was a kindly appearing colonel who saw to it that the girl was given her favorite cold drink—an iced Coca-Cola—before he began speaking with her.

"You have seen much of communism, Andrea," he said. "Tell me, *ma chérie,* what is your opinion of the Viet Minh, the Viet Cong, and the Pathet Lao?"

Andrea took a sip of her drink, then pointed at the man's pistol in the holster on his hip. "Let me have your gun, monsieur, and I will kill every one of them."

"I am afraid that would be impossible," the colonel said. "Even a big soldier could not kill all of them by himself. But there is another way you can fight them."

Andrea, eager, leaned forward. "How, monsieur?"

"You have some very unusual talents and bits of knowledge, Andrea," the colonel said. "Those things, when combined with others that we could teach you, would make you a most effective fighter against the communists."

"What could you teach me, monsieur?" Andrea asked.

"Well, for example, you know three languages. Would you like to learn more? Tai, Chinese, possibly English?"

"If that would help me kill Pathet Lao and Viet Cong," Andrea said, "then I would want to learn. But I don't understand how that would do anything to destroy those Red devils."

"These would be skills you could learn—along with others—that would enable you to go into their midst and do mischief and harm to them," the

110

colonel said. "But learning these things would be difficult and unpleasant at times."

"What could be more difficult and unpleasant than what I've already been through?" Andrea asked.

"A good point," the colonel said. He recognized the maturity in the young girl and decided to speak to her as an adult. "When would you like to begin this new phase in your education, mademoiselle?"

"Now! Today!" Andrea cried, getting to her feet.

"I am sorry, mademoiselle," the colonel said with a smile. "You will have to wait until tomorrow morning."

The next day's training was the first part of two solid years of intensified schooling. South Vietnamese intelligence decided to have the young girl retain the name of Thuy—as the *Soeurs de la Charité* had named her—to mask her true identity from the Reds.

Andrea acquired more languages along with unusual skills necessary in the dangerous profession she had chosen for herself. Besides disguises and a talented skill at mimicking various accents and dialects, the fast-maturing girl learned various methods of how to kill people. These included poisons and drugs, easily concealable weapons, and the less subtle method of blowing an adversary to bits with plastic explosive. After each long day of training, Andrea concluded her schedule by poring over books of mug shots and portraits showing the faces and identities of communist leaders and officials up in the north.

Finally, with her deadly education completed,

seventeen-year-old Andrea Thuy neé Roget, went out into the cold.

During two years of operations, she assassinated four top Red bigwigs. Her devotion to their destruction was such that she was even willing to use her body if it would lower their guard and aid her in gaining their confidence. Once that was done, Andrea displayed absolutely no reluctance in administering the coup de grâce to put an end to their efforts at spreading world communism.

When the American involvement in South Vietnam stepped up, a Central Intelligence Agency case officer named Clayton Andrews learned of this unusual young woman and her deadly talents. Andrews had been tasked with creating an elite killer/raider outfit. After learning of Andrea he knew he wanted her to be a part of this crack team. Using his influence and talents of persuasion, he saw to it that the beautiful female operative was sent to Langley Air Force Base in Virginia to the special CIA school located there.

When the Americans finished honing her fangs at Langley, she returned to South Vietnam and was put into another job category. Commissioned a lieutenant in the ARVN, she was appointed a temporary major and assigned to Special Operation Group's Black Eagles Detachment, which was under the command of Captain Robert Falconi.

Andrea accompanied the Black Eagles on their first mission. This operation, named Hanoi Hellground, was a direct action type against a Red whorehouse and pleasure palace deep within North Vietnam. Andrea participated in the deadly combat

112

that resulted, killing her share of the Red enemy in the firefights that erupted in the green hell of the jungle. There was not a Black Eagle who would deny she had been superlative in the performance of her duties.

But she soon fell out of grace.

Not because of cowardice, sloppy work, or inefficiency, but because of that one thing that could disarm any woman—love. She went head over heels into it with Robert Falconi.

Clayton Andrews was promoted upstairs, and his place was taken by another CIA case officer. This one, named Chuck Fagin, found he had inherited a damned good outfit, except that its commander and one of the operatives were involved in a red-hot romance. An emotional entanglement like that spelled disaster with a capital D in the espionage and intelligence business. It was a situation that could not be tolerated.

Fagin had no choice but to pull Andrea out of active ops. He put her in his office as the administrative director. Andrea did not protest. Deep in her heart she knew that the decision was the right one. She would have done the same thing. She or Falconi might have lost their heads and pulled something emotional or thoughtless if either one had suddenly been placed into a dangerous situation. That sort of illogical condition could have resulted not only in their own deaths, but the demise of other Black Eagles as well. At times a dedicated operative had to be tough on herself.

She went out into the cold twice more after that, however; once during operations with a Chinese

113

mercenary guerrilla unit, and again when captured by communist agents and taken north. This final episode ended with her rescue by Falconi. When she returned to South Vietnam, she'd been sent stateside to recuperate and be retrained.

Now, once again worried about others in her charge, Andrea Thuy was in the hands of the people she hated the most in the world.

CHAPTER 9

Colonel Dimitri Sogolov lay on his sweat-soaked bed in the Russian Embassy in downtown Hanoi. It was three o'clock in the morning but he was wide awake, unable to sleep in the weather that to him was hot and oppressive. When he'd first retired for the night, he'd done so in a pair of pajamas. But, after an hour of tossing and turning in perspiring restlessness, Sogolov finally stripped down to the buff. Even the rain falling outside did nothing to give him physical comfort.

His arrival for a duty posting in North Vietnam's capital city had taken place only three days before. The Russian had been as flabbergasted by the unceasing falling rain as he had been at the sight of Vietnamese wearing sweaters in what he considered sweltering weather.

Sogolov was a KGB officer. His assignment had nothing to do with military matters unless they affected the state security of Mother Russia. The duties the colonel would perform would take him into the shadowy secret-police world of his profession. It was an environment of subterfuge, denouncements of individuals, spying and ruthless violations of human rights. But, because of acute physical discomfort, Sogolov gave no thought to work.

He finally got out of bed and walked over to the open window. Outside, in the small courtyard, the rain continued to fall without interruption. The colonel stuck his hand out to feel the water. It felt warm enough to bathe in. He sighed and leaned against the sill, damning the luck that had brought him to such a land. His KGB colleagues back in Moscow headquarters who had been stationed in southeast Asia had said little of the heat when they described the duty area to him. Instead, they spoke glowingly of the small, beautiful women and the exquisite way they made love. Sogolov had looked forward to such sexual experiences, but he was so damned hot and tired that he didn't even have the energy to request one of the state-sponsored concubines for the night.

He went back to his bed and sat down. A bottle of vodka sat on the table next to him. He picked it up and treated himself to a big gulp. A damp pack of Rosidarstvo cigarettes next received his attention. He pulled one from the package and stuck the loosely rolled fag in his mouth. He lit it and took a dry, burning drag. A coughing fit hit him and he smashed out the butt in the ashtray by the vodka.

A knock on the door interrupted his solitary misery. *"Tovarisch Podkovnik?"* a muffled voice asked from the hallway outside.

116

"Da?" Sogolov answered. "What is it?"

"The comrade general wants you to report to him immediately."

Sogolov checked his watch to make sure of the time. He knew the summons would be damned important. "I am on my way," comrade," he said. He quickly dressed in the light-khaki uniform bearing the royal-blue epaulets of the KGB. After slipping into his shoes, he hurried out of his room and made his way down the dimly lit stairs to the bottom floor. He had to walk through the entire building before he reached General Kuznetz's office door. He rapped loudly on the thick portal.

"Enter!"

Sogolov presented himself and saluted sharply. "Comrade General, I beg to report as ordered."

KGB General Josef Kuznetz sat at his desk that faced the doorway. He returned the salute. "Welcome to Hanoi, Comrade Colonel."

"Spasibo, Comrade General," Sogolov replied.

"I apologize both for not seeing you sooner and also for the inconvenience of the hour," the general said.

"I am not disturbed by either condition, Comrade General," Sogolov properly replied.

Kuznetz carefully studied the man. "You are somewhat different from your predecessor."

"Do you mean Krashchenko, Comrade General?" Sogolov asked. "He is an old pal of mine. I've not seen him for years."

"He has fallen on the field of honor," Kuznetz said.

Sogolov only nodded. The disappearance of KGB

men was not all that unusual. If a death occurred during a clandestine operation, the cause of the man's demise could be listed as anything from heart failure to an automobile accident. If he'd fallen into serious disfavor, his assassination would be treated in the same manner.

Either way—it was not wise to inquire too deeply into what Mother Russia did not wish to reveal.

Kuznetz lit a cigarette and offered one to Sogolov. The general exhaled a thick cloud of smoke. "During your briefing for this assignment, were you apprised of an American unit known as the Black Eagles?"

Sogolov shrugged. "I was only told there were certain enemy formations that had proven particularly troublesome in the Vietnamese War of Liberation. There were no names mentioned."

"I see," the general said. "Then allow me to elaborate. An American lieutenant colonel named Robert Falconi is the commander of a detachment of particularly nasty fellows. They call themselves the Black Eagles. They have thwarted several important operations. This even includes the KGB. As a matter of fact, Falconi and the Black Eagles are responsible for your old friend Krashchenko's death."

"*Vnevrayenie!*" Sogolov cursed.

"Another interesting point is that Falconi is a Soviet citizen," Kuznetz added.

"A traitor?" Sogolov asked, dumbfounded.

"By our law," the general said. "His mother was born in the Soviet Union—a Jewess who betrayed

118

communism and went to America."

"I understand," Sogolov said. "If we could get our hands on this Falconi and bring him back to the Soviet Union we could put him on trial as a treasonous war criminal, *nyet?*"

"*Da.*" Kuznetz answered in the affirmative. "Now let me bring you up to date. A few weeks ago, a Viet Cong commander named Nygoyen Li requested permission to launch a quite unusual operation against an American Green Beret camp called Nui Dep. There were also some South Vietnamese militiamen and their families there."

Sogolov glanced out the barred window at the dark rainy night. "The comrade Viet Cong officer wanted to attack in this weather?"

"Yes. I was against it as was the Soviet Army adviser, but Nygoyen Li presented a good argument that the assault would succeed because it would be totally unexpected."

"I suppose," Sogolov said hesitantly.

"By all logic it should have," Kuznetz said. "But the entire affair turned out to be a complete failure. The Viet Cong suffered heavy losses and were routed."

Sogolov nodded. "Am I to assume the Black Eagles were involved?"

"Of course," Kuznetz said. "They were there in force and played a leading role in the defeat our comrades suffered. But we did come out ahead on one count."

"The Black Eagles were destroyed in the attack?" Sogolov asked.

"Hardly," Kuznetz scoffed. "But we captured three nurses from the camp."

"That does not seem important," Sogolov said.

"Normally, it would not be," the general said. "But one of the nurses was the sweetheart of a Black Eagle and the other is one of their wives."

"Ah!" Sogolov exclaimed. "Things are looking up for us. What about the third woman?"

"We think," Kuznetz said carefully, "that she is Andrea Thuy."

"Andrea Thuy!" Sogolov exclaimed. "She was given a great deal of coverage in my mission briefing. Are you sure we have her in our hands?"

"No, unfortunately," Kuznetz said. "We must make a positive identification. The woman was once our prisoner, but Falconi and his men rescued her."

"It is thought that she and Falconi are lovers."

"Correct. So, if we have her, he will once again come looking for his lady love," Kuznetz said. "That is where you will come in."

"Yes, Comrade General. I am ready for whatever duties are assigned me," Sogolov responded. "But allow me to suggest that all care be given to this prisoner. If indeed it is Andrea Thuy, she may commit suicide if she thinks she is compromised."

"This has been taken into consideration," Kuznetz said. "The Viet Cong comrades are being very subtle and careful with her."

"That is comforting to hear, Comrade General."

"Nygoyen Li and the women are far out in the jungle," Kuznetz said. "You are to travel south and link up with them at a place called Ben Quang. There

120

you will examine the nurse we suspect of being Andrea Thuy. If you are positive it is she—and you must be certain to the point of having no doubts— we will set up a most enterprising trap for Falconi and his Black Eagles."

"Will I have a guide, Comrade General?"

"Yes. A North Vietnamese Army general named Truong Van will act as your liaison," Kuznetz explained. "He speaks fluent Russian and French. As a matter of fact, he was a special aide to your friend Krashchenko."

"Very well, Comrade General," Sogolov said. "When do I leave?"

"General Truong is waiting for you in the foyer of the embassy, Comrade Colonel," Kuznetz said. *"Proshanie!"*

"Goodbye, Comrade General!"

Nygoyen Li's intelligence officer was an old campaigner named Nugent. A hardcore, dedicated communist in spite of coming from a wealthy family, he'd been educated in Paris. While studying the classics in music, art, and literature, Nugent hung around with a radical left-wing element of the student body. These socialists influenced his political leanings to the extent that he was a fervent Marxist by the time he returned to French Indochina just before the outbreak of World War II. He fought as a line soldier against the Japanese, but by the time the Viet Minh revolution began, his superior education and intellect had earned him staff positions.

Now, most of his work consisted of getting briefed by higher headquarters on intelligence regarding South Vietnamese and American activities. Nugent would then make sure the company commanders and platoon leaders were given the necessary information before operations. The only interrogation he did was with occasional prisoners of war. These sessions were mainly made up of questions interspersed with kicks and punches until the captive either told all he knew or convinced Nugent that he knew nothing or was not going to talk.

The end result was the same: The prisoner was executed.

But the nurses presented a special problem. No doubt he could beat the hell out of them and get what he wanted in the way of information. But what if the upper echelons were upset by bruised, bleeding merchandise? On the other hand, if he made no effort at all, those same staff officers would rake him over the coals and he would be toting heavy shells as an ammunition bearer for some fast-moving youthful mortar crew.

Nugent decided to split the difference: He would threaten them, but do nothing.

The first prisoner was the American. To the small Oriental man, she seemed large and gangly. Much like the French women of his student days. Her blond hair and blue eyes so unnerved him, that he only managed a few questions through an interpreter before he sent her away and sent for one of the Vietnamese nurses.

Nugent knew they were all important, but he

didn't know why. He tried a line of questioning that would make the woman reveal a lot about herself, but all he learned was that she was a nurse at Nui Dep and came from the village of Tam Nuroc. There was no language barrier and she protested about the children's mothers being taken away, and that the young ones were getting sicker. She complained so much that she reminded Nugent of his wife.

He cut that session off quickly, too.

The third was the Vietnamese woman who had a strange way about her. She was as tall as he was. Her skin and eyes were Oriental in certain ways but Occidental in others. Nugent thought her exotic. When he began his questioning, he started at a very basic level:

"Yen co la gi?" he asked.

"My name is Co Dow," Andrea Thuy calmly answered.

He continued speaking to her and noting her answers. Finally, he realized she was Eurasian. Nugent carried on as before, then suddenly asked, *"Voulez-vous une tasse de thé?"*

Andrea smiled sweetly. *"Toi khong hieu,"* she replied to the question in French. "I do not understand."

"It is not important," Nugent said, reverting back to Vietnamese. "Where are your parents from, Miss Dow?"

"Saigon," Andrea said, continuing her cover story. "My father owns a pharmacy there."

"I see," Nugent said. "Who is European? Your mother or your father?"

"Neither one," Andrea asked. "Why do you ask such a question?"

"I can tell by your eyes that you are not pure Asian," Nugent said, not attempting to hide his racist attitude that was so typical of Vietnamese society.

Andrea feigned shame. "My maternal grandfather was a French soldier who seduced my grandmother. I never met him."

"Such disgrace!" Nugent said.

Andrea nodded, covering her face with her hands. "My father was disowned by his family when he married my mother."

"I am not surprised," Nugent said. He gestured a dismissal. "You may leave, Miss Dow. I have no more questions to ask of you."

"I hope your commander will show mercy on the children," Andrea said, relieved that she'd slipped through the interrogation grin unscathed.

"The comrade battalion commander will know what to do," Nugent said. "Do not worry." He watched her walk back through the dripping jungle under the escort of two young Viet Cong fighters. When she was out of sight, Nugent turned and went directly to the command post. He stepped inside the large poncho that was stretched out to act as a crude roof. *"Chao ong,"* Nugent greeted Nygoyen Li. "Greetings, Comrade Battalion Commander."

"And greetings to you, Comrade Staff Officer," Nygoyen Li said. "How did your interrogations go?"

"I have completed the task, Comrade Battalion Commander," Nugent answered.

"And what is your estimate of the prisoners?"

"Two are unremarkable, but the third is unusual," Nugent answered.

"What interests you in her, comrade?" Nygoyen Li asked.

"Comrade Battalion Commander," Nugent said, "she is Andrea Thuy."

CHAPTER 10

The Viet Cong radio operator strained to hear the weak signal that his wornout commo set bleeped at him through the old taped earphones on his head.

Everyone within the immediate vicinity of the command post had been ordered to complete silence. But the monsoon neither hears or obeys the mandates of puny men, so the rain continued to splatter down, making a racket all its own.

But finally the message was received.

"Comrade Battalion Commander, the transmission is complete," the radio operator said, ripping the page from his notebook. He handed the message over.

Nygoyen Li perused the missive carefully. "We are to deliver the prisoners immediately to the special committee at a point south of Ben Quang," he announced to the assembled company commanders. "There is a good chance that a particularly nasty group of American gangsters are pursuing us in a desperate attempt to rescue the women. That must

127

not happen." He paused and looked meaningfully at his officers, then repeated, "That must *not* happen!"

"*Co,* Comrade Battalion Commander!" they shouted in unison.

"Therefore, I am going to dispatch Comrade Company Commander Khung's men as rear guard. They are to remain in constant contact with the pursuers, pressuring them constantly to keep them moving at a slow pace. If Khung sustains heavy casualties, then I will assign him more men from the other companies."

Khung, happy for this chance to redeem himself after the mauling at Camp Nui Dep, smiled. "I am honored, Comrade Battalion Commander! Even now I have dispatched a platoon to lie in wait for any running dogs who would dare track us."

"*Duoc roi!*" Nygoyen Li said. "I now appoint Comrade Staff Officer Nugent as commander of a special guard to watch the women. That group will move north without delay until we meet up with the special committee. The others will remain between both groups, ready to support anyone in trouble. Is this all understood?"

"*Co,* Comrade Battalion Commander!"

Archie Dobbs could sense the presence of other men ahead of him in the jungle. Not even the heavy atmosphere of falling rain could dull his senses of direction and impending danger.

Such a talent was as natural to Archie Dobbs as breathing. The young man was a born tracker and pathfinder.

128

If he had come into the world a couple of hundred years earlier, the intrepid corporal would have been among the first to break across the Appalachian or Allegheny mountains. He would have been a companion of Daniel Boone and his ilk during the great migrations west to explore the dangerous wilderness that spread out from the narrow seaboard of civilization. Archie would have loved to be the first to explore across the unknown sprawl of the American continent. Archie's ancestors, who had arrived in the Colonies during the times when such activities were feasible, had been prevented from becoming pioneers because of the circumstances of their arrival.

They had come in chains, released from English prisons as bonded servants—virtual slaves to the people who held papers on them. Any attempt to leave the supervision and control of their masters was a serious crime. Confused and locked into a cruel system, they had no choice but to exist within the cruel mandates of the system. No man would escape even tyranny if it meant leaving his wife and children behind. In truth, they were as locked into slavery as the unfortunate blacks on southern plantations. After several generations, the former bonded servants, through circumstances brought on by the industrial revolution, were caught up in the manufacturing syndrome and life-style of the East Coast.

Thus, the Dobbses—like many other families—donated several generations to the mills and factories of Massachusetts.

Archie's older ancestors in England had been

involved in more romantic activities to earn their bread. In fact, their way of making a living delivered them to the English judicial system that eventually sold the freebooting bunch into cruel bondage in the Colonies.

The Dobbs family were poachers.

No earl, duke, lord of a manor, or even the King of England could keep the persistent Dobbs clan from hunting and fishing their private domains. Generations of following this dangerous trade had developed genes in which the necessary skills of stealth, tracking, and directional orientation were utilized to the maximum. Fathers passed this unlawful trade down to their sons, until the craft seemed a part of their genetic heritage.

These talents were combined with stubbornness and fearlessness, too.

To this day in the English county of Nottinghamshire a tale is told out of the misty past about a man named Crompton Dobbs who, rather than shrieking in agony while being drawn and quartered, shouted of how he had enjoyed the lord's roasted venison—the very crime for which he was being so painfully executed.

Now the scion of that great line of interloping outdoorsmen prowled through a rain-soaked tropical forest, looking for the most dangerous of game to hunt—other men.

Blue Richards was the scout's closest contact with the rest of the detachment. When the Alabamian saw Archie's hand-and-arm signal to halt, he immediately passed it back to the rest of the Black Eagles.

Archie, ignoring the cold discomfort of the dripping palm bushes, crouched down and moved forward at a crawl. He stopped every four or five yards to wait and listen, letting his instincts guide him.

Finally, he spotted what had caused him so much nervousness.

Several Viet Cong, hastily concealed in the jungle growth, waited in tense anticipation a few meters ahead of Archie. The scout slowly pulled back, then stood up and hurried to the rear to find Lieutenant Colonel Robert Falconi.

Falconi, after halting with the rest of the detachment, had waited with his top men—Lieutenant Ray Swift Elk and Sergeant Major Top Gordon—for their recon man to return and report whatever it was that had caught his attention.

When Archie arrived, his eyes were lit with excitement. "Sir, there's a Charlie ambush up ahead about twenty-five or thirty meters. The sonofabitches are spread across in a single line."

"Mmm," Falconi mused. "That means they weren't real sure just what route we'd be coming in on."

"It kinda worries me, though," Top said. "How come they ain't running like hell after we kicked their butts back at Nui Dep?"

Ray Swift Elk offered a suggestion. "Maybe they figure we'll come after 'em for sure since they ran off with those women and kids."

"It doesn't matter one way or the other," Falconi said. "They're out there, and we're going to kick the little bastards' asses. Now here's the poop: Calvin

131

and Malpractice will hit the line on the left. I want Paulo and Gunnar to do the same thing on the right. The rest of us will go straight ahead, then after we hit the line we'll split 'em up and devour the portions individually. It should go fast and easy if they're positioned as Archie said."

"Great idea, sir," Swift Elk said.

"Okay. Once the flanks are engaged and we've slammed into the center of the line, Archie and I'll veer left, and you and Top go to the right. That way the VC should be kicked apart for easier pickings."

"Let's do it to 'em," Archie said impatiently.

"Right," Falconi said. "Ray. Top. Go get the men ready. We've got a war to fight."

The Soviet UAZ-69A command car rolled along the rain-slicked macadam highway at a careful fifty kilometers an hour. The driver, a youthful North Vietnamese soldier, was acutely aware of keeping the ride as smooth as possible for his two important passengers.

In the backseat, sweating profusely despite his light clothing, KGB Colonel Dimitri Sogolov pulled a handkerchief from his pocket and mopped his brow. He glanced at the officer beside him. The man seemed sullen as hell, but Sogolov decided to try some friendly conversation. "This is beautiful country, Comrade General. So green and lush."

NVA General Truong Van looked briefly at his companion. "It is typical of monsoon country." Truong was mad as hell. He'd thought his promotion to the rank of general meant more responsibility and privileges. He'd spent two years serving as a liaison lackey to another KGB man, but at least they'd been the same rank. Now he was forced to toady up to a damned Russian colonel who was his subordinate in military grade.

Sogolov lit a cigarette. "I understand you served with Colonel Krashchenko," he remarked almost as if he were reading Truong's mind.

"Yes," Truong answered curtly. Then he fought down a smile and said, "He died for the glory of Marxism."

"So I've been informed. Actually, I hadn't seen Gregori for several years," Sogolov said. "How did he keep himself?"

Truong now lit his own smoke. "He worked hard on defeating the Black Eagles. He had a particular hatred for Lieutenant Colonel Robert Falconi."

"I see," Sogolov said. "Krashchenko was like a wolfhound. Once he sank his teeth into a project, he wouldn't let go under any circumstances."

"I imagine he let go quickly when the Black Eagles blew him to hell down south," Truong said.

"*Shto*—what?" Sogolov hadn't realized that his old comrade had actually been sent down into South Vietnam.

Truong nervously flicked the ash off his cigarette. The information on the true facts regarding the demise of Krashchenko was highly classified. He hoped he hadn't made a security faux pas. "I thought you had been fully briefed, Comrade Colonel," he said with a hint of sarcasm in his voice.

Sogolov did not miss the unfriendly tone. "I have not been in North Vietnam long, Comrade General.

Since I will be brought up to date eventually anyway, perhaps you will be kind enough to give me all the facts as you know them."

"Krashchenko formed a group similar to the Black Eagles," Truong said in way of a brief explanation. "The unit, called the Red Bears, was trained in your country. They were Russians, Poles, Czechs, Bulgarians—all white men."

Sogolov almost sneered as his mind thought, *Of course, you little yellow bastard!* But his voice said, "I am sure there was a good reason for that. There are many elite units in the Russian forces as well as those of the Warsaw Pact countries."

Truong tossed his cigarette out the narrow opening of the window beside him. "They lost."

"Perhaps the Black Eagles will lose this time, Comrade General," Sogolov suggested. "After all, it appears that we have Andrea Thuy in our hands."

"She has been a prisoner before," Truong reminded him.

"Yes, Comrade General, but the KGB was not involved in that particular instance."

Truong, angrier than ever, lit another cigarette and glared out the rain-splattered window.

Noise was not a problem as the Black Eagles moved rapidly forward in their attack. The rain made enough of a racket to cover any sound. Falconi, farther ahead than the others, was the first to come into contact with the Viet Cong.

His M16 kicked back with every pull on the trigger. The first rounds clipped off broad leaves of jungle flora before ripping into the VC positions. Within a split second, Archie, Top, and Ray Swift Elk's own weapons spewed out fusillades that joined their commanding officer's.

Over on the left flank, Calvin Culpepper cut loose with a salvo to cover his old friend Malpractice McCorckel. Malpractice took advantage of the situation to advance to a position offering him a good field of fire. Now he hosed out steady streams of full automatic fire while Calvin quickly but carefully moved into a more advantageous location. When this was accomplished, the pair of Black Eagles were well situated to blow the hell out of that side of the line.

Meanwhile, over on the right, Gunnar Olson and Paulo Garcia had run into a snag. A Charlie machine gun had been positioned there, and the gunner knew his job. He kept up a steady, rhythmic enfilade fire that smacked heavy slugs into the trees around the two men.

With his face pressed down into the soft jungle mud, an angry Paulo Garcia cursed his luck. He could barely see Gunnar through the vegetation a few meters away. Paulo waved and uttered a low whistle.

Gunnar looked toward him. "Yeah?"

"When that bastard swings the other way, I'm gonna make a move. Cover me."

"You got it, pal," Gunnar said. He pushed the selector on his weapon to full-auto. As soon as the bullets zipping past overhead shifted a bit, Gunnar cut loose with a long fireburst that emptied his thirty-round magazine.

Meanwhile, Paulo got up on all fours and scurried forward. At the same time, he pulled a grenade off his harness. Then he leaped to his feet and threw hard, immediately dropping back to the ground.

The explosion was followed by a loud scream. Paulo and Gunnar both leaped to their feet and charged forward, sending intertwined volleys of fire ahead of them. When they reached the objective, they found two dead VC. An overturned Soviet light machine gun was lying on top of their bodies.

Gunnar picked up the heavy weapon and examined it. Except for a few shrapnel scratches from Paulo's grenade, it was in fine working order. "It looks like I'm back in the machine-gun business, Paulo. Thanks."

"My pleasure," Paulo responded. "Now let's move in toward the center and finish this attack."

Falconi and the three men with him had smashed the middle part of the Viet Cong line. Now, splitting off, they all moved toward the flanks—Falconi and Archie going left, and Ray and Top attacking to the right.

A few more sporadic shots followed as the Black Eagle detachment linked up per their commander's plan. The result of the coordinated assault was a dozen dead Viet Cong, their sprawled bodies becoming soaked by the monsoon rain.

Top gathered up everyone and brought them in toward the spot where Falconi and Ray Swift Elk waited. When all were present, Falconi looked upward at the black, cloudy sky. "We won't be getting any aerial supply support on this one, guys, and we'll soon be out of ammunition for these M16s. It looks like we're back to using commie equipment."

"Yes, sir," Archie said. "I know what's coming. We'll be picking up these dead Charlies' AK47 rifles and ammo pouches, right?"

"It won't be the first time the VC are our S4s," Top Gordon said with a grin.

"There's a light machine gun back there," Gunnar said, pointing in the direction where he and Paulo had launched the coordinated grenade attack. "I'd be real proud to tote that baby."

"If it's the right caliber," Falconi said. "I don't want any ammo supply problems."

"She's just like the one I left back at Nui Dep," Gunnar said. "An RPK 7.62-millimeter. The only difference is it's got box magazines instead of 75-round drums. But they hold a nifty forty rounds, so I'll be able to get by pretty good."

"Go for it," Falconi said, knowing Gunnar's preference for heavier gunnery.

Top glared at the others still standing around. "What the hell are you jokers waiting for? Get your butts over to them VC stiffs and pick up weapons and ammo. Let's go!"

The Black Eagles came to life at the familiar sound of Top's irritated voice. They each went to a dead Viet Cong and took the man's weapon and ammo pouches. When they were fully equipped, the detachment reported back to the sergeant major.

"Okay," Top said. "Let's break the American taxpayers' hearts."

Each M16 rifle was taken by its owner and smashed against the trunk of a heavy tree. A deep hole was dug in the ground in which these broken weapons, along with extra 5.56 millimeter ammunition, were thrown in.

Top got the white phosphorous grenade he'd carried in his patrol pack. He pulled the pin and dropped it into the excavation. The device hissed and belched white burning shrapnel as it exploded bullets and turned carefully machined gun metal into molten hunks of useless iron.

Even the persistent monsoon rains could not quench the hell of that manmade device.

CHAPTER 11

The three nurses put the finishing touches on the temporary shelter they had constructed for the night. Andrea watched Betty Lou slip the last palm frond into place on the latticelike structure.

"You're becoming quite expert at this," Andrea said.

"Yes," Jean said, echoing the opinion. "You are as good at it as we are."

"I have a couple of expert teachers," Betty Lou responded.

The ladies were a cosmetologist's nightmare. Their hair, exposed so long to the monsoon weather, was damp and stringy. The nurses' fatigue uniforms had deteriorated to torn, shapeless sacks. All traces of makeup had washed away, leaving their faces plain and nearly colorless.

But their personal appearance was the last thing on their collective minds.

"Let's see to the children," Betty Lou said.

They went under the palm roof, where the

children were resting. Andrea, while well trained in first aid and emergency medical treatment, was far from having the expertise of the two nurses. She stayed out of the way as her two friends went from child to child, speaking softly in comforting tones as they examined the sick kids.

With no medical instruments, Betty Lou and Jean relied on feeling little foreheads to check for fever. They tried to tend to the task without upsetting their small patients. They used tender pats and caresses to check temperature and pulses. The children cuddled close to the women, enjoying the solace and warmth of being next to their bodies.

"They all have fevers," Betty Lou said sadly.

"Yes," Jean agreed. "And weak pulses. I am worried." She held an infant in her arms. "Especially this one. He is so sick, I think he is in danger without medicine."

"God!" Betty Lou said. "We must get them out of this cold and wet."

Andrea watched the incomplete but affectionate treatment being administered to the children. Finally, anger surging up from her soul into her conscious mind, she turned and went outside the lean-to. *"Nguoi linh!"* she said sharply to the guard. "I must speak to your commander."

The sentry, a soft-eyed youngster with a kindly face, shrugged apologetically. *"Toi tiec,"* he said. "I cannot do that."

Andrea pointed inside to the children. "Those little ones are very sick. If they are not helped, they will die. Now! I demand to speak to your officer in charge."

The Viet Cong looked at the kids, then into Andrea's angry face. He sighed. "I will see what I can do." He motioned his comrade to move closer and watch the women. Then he hurried away.

Betty Lou came outside. "What good do you think that will do?"

"As the old saying goes, 'It couldn't hurt,'" Andrea said in a determined tone of voice.

Fifteen minutes later, to the nurses' surprise, the young guard returned, with Battalion Commander Nygoyen Li walking ahead of him. The VC officer was plainly annoyed. "What is going on?"

"These children have grown sicker," Andrea said firmly. "They must be helped with medicine and blankets."

"I have no such supplies for my own men," Nygoyen Li said.

"Do you intend to let these children die?" Jean asked.

"I have no intention of harming them," Nygoyen Li said a bit defensively. "Whatever good or bad luck they have is no concern or responsibility of mine."

"If you cannot give them proper medical treatment," Andrea said, "then please leave us here. Why do you insist on dragging us with you?"

"I have definite orders," Nygoyen Li said.

Andrea, becoming exceedingly suspicious, caged her question. "Do you mean, Battalion Commander, that your superiors have given you direct orders to take three women and a group of sick

141

children as prisoners of war?"

Nygoyen Li avoided a direct answer. "I have my orders. There is no point in you complaining. Do not bother me again." He turned and walked rapidly away.

The young Viet Cong guard watched his commander depart. He looked back at Andrea. "It is sad," he said.

"Yes," Andrea agreed.

The guerrilla pulled his poncho off the Chinese cartridge belt he wore. "You may take this, if you wish."

Andrea had noticed the piece of equipment before. She examined it. "This is American."

"Yes," the VC said proudly. "I was awarded it for bravery in battle."

Andrea nodded. The Viet Cong, pushed hard for good equipment, gave away such items that were common issue in regular armies as medals for valor.

"Cam on ong—thank you," Andrea said. It was a very generous gift. "It will make an excellent ground cloth for the children to sleep on."

"Duoc roi," he said with a smile. "My name is Dhang. I will help you when I can."

Andrea, sincerely grateful, wasted no time in getting the poncho inside. Now the children would be off the wet ground. Perhaps some small lives would be saved. But her initial pleasure faded away with the realization of a newer situation that could prove ominous for her.

The Viet Cong commander's orders to keep them as prisoners was perplexing. Unless the reason behind it was to get her back into communist captivity.

The automobile trip shared by KGB Colonel Dimitri Sogolov and General Truong Van of the North Vietnamese Army had drifted into strained silence.

Their young driver, who could not understand either the Russian or French language in which the officers conversed, could still easily tell the two were not getting along. He noted a road sign as they drove past it. He made a remark in Vietnamese.

"What did he say?" asked Sogolov.

"He is reminding us that we are to stop at the military intelligence bureau at Dong Hoi."

"Ah, *koroshi*," Sogolov said. "How far is it?"

Truong leaned toward the driver. *"Tu day den Dong Hoi bao xa?"* When the man answered, Truong said curtly, "Twenty kilometers."

The journey continued in silence as the small auto traveled down the wet highway, throwing up streams of water. When they arrived on the outskirts of Dong Hoi, the driver was forced to slow down and lean on his horn as he maneuvered in and out of bicycle, ox-cart, and pedestrian traffic. He suddenly whipped off onto a side street and picked up speed for a few moments before slamming on the brakes in front of a building.

Two NVA guards, standing under the shelter of an overhanging wooden awning, saluted sharply. One stepped out into the rain and opened the door

143

for the officers.

Truong led the way out, going quickly inside the building. He had obviously been there before. He went down a hallway, then straight into an office door. Sogolov, being a taller man with longer legs, had no trouble in keeping up.

Inside the room, a major of the intelligence service saluted. *"Bienvenu,"* he said in French. "Welcome to the Dong Hoi Military District Headquarters," he then said politely in English. "I have ordered hot coffee."

"You knew when we would arrive?" Sogolov asked.

"Excuse me, Comrade Colonel," the major said. "I have men at strategic points around the city on a twenty-four-hour basis. I was telephoned fifteen minute ago that you had arrived."

"Very commendable," Truong said, pleased. "The North Vietnamese Army can be quite efficient at times."

"So I see," Sogolov said.

A rather plump young female soldier appeared with a tray of coffee. Both officers gave her a close scrutiny. Truong thought she looked like a fat cow, but Sogolov was aroused by the sight of her ample behind. This was the kind of woman he liked—a good, stout peasant lass with a wide pelvis to push back against the strong thrusts of her lovers.

The girl was aware of the Russian's lust-filled stare. After pouring the cups of coffee and serving them, she made a hasty, nervous exit.

"What is the latest situation with the Viet Cong unit that attacked Nui Dep?" Truong asked, taking a

144

sip of the hot brew.

"Our latest reports are but hours old," the major replied. "They indicate that the Black Eagle gangsters are still in hot pursuit. Falconi and his men ripped apart an ambush and massacred the brave Viet Cong who attempted to stop them."

"The comrades seem to be getting a rough handling by those Americans," Sogolov said.

Truong felt a flash of anger. "Yes. Almost as badly as your friend Krashchenko and his Red Bears."

Sogolov avoided any open reply to the obvious sarcasm, but he filed it away for future reference. Instead, he spoke directly to the major. "Kindly radio department headquarters and inform them that they are to dispatch a reinforced company of North Vietnamese infantry into the operational area to deal with Falconi."

Truong's ire did not abate. He strongly resented the authority enjoyed by the Russian colonel. Even he, as a North Vietnamese general, did not enjoy such a prestigious position in his own country.

"Yes, Comrade Colonel," the major said. "I also wish to inform you that the comrade intelligence officer with the Viet Cong unit is strongly convinced that one of the women is most certainly Andrea Thuy."

Sogolov's eyes widened. "Is she that well known?"

"Oh, yes," the major said. "Both the North Vietnamese and Viet Cong forces have been advised of her existence. They are under orders to maintain a constant vigilance for her presence. If she is in their hands and does not realize she has been compromised, then we will have scored a great coup."

"The longer this situation drags on, the more chance there is she will become suspicious," Sogolov said. "We cannot allow her to escape or commit suicide. Hasten that radio message, if you please, Comrade Major."

"Mais oui, Camarade Colonel!"

With the interview over, Sogolov and Truong returned to the car. "We will go directly to Ben Quang," Truong said to the driver. As the car turned around, he looked at Sogolov. "Why don't we simply have the other women and children turned loose, and bring out Andrea Thuy directly?"

"There is a propaganda coup to be scored here, Comrade General," Sogolov said. "And a tactical victory of sorts, too. If we can keep Falconi and his Black Eagles in a hot, emotional pursuit we will be able to eventually bring them to ground like hunted foxes. In order to do this, we must dangle Andrea Thuy in front of their noses."

"I agree," Truong said. "But what about those nurses and children?"

"That is the propaganda of which I speak," Sogolov said. "We will display them to the world's press as war victims that the brave Viet Cong comrades have rescued from the Green Beret fascists at Camp Nui Dep." The Russian smiled. "Either way, Falconi will either die or be our prisoner."

Betty Lou took a deep breath and sighed. She wiped at the tears in her eyes as she gently placed her hand on the cold brow of the baby. "The little one died," she said softly.

146

Andrea and Jean left the other children they were tending and came over to kneel down by the dead child. Suddenly Andrea leaped up and stepped outside the lean-to. She spoke angrily and firmly to Dhang who stood guard.

"Fetch *Thie Ta* Nygoyen Li now!"

Dhang shook his head. "With respect, but *khong co!*" he said. "The comrade battalion commander was most explicit that I was not to annoy him about you."

"A little baby has died," Andrea said. "More will surely follow unless he helps them."

"I have my orders," Dhang insisted.

"Does a brave Viet Cong help murder children?" Andrea asked.

"Of course not," Dhang said. "I am fighting to liberate my land from the capitalist oppressors and their running dogs in South Vietnam."

Andrea eyed him closely. "Did you volunteer for the Viet Cong?"

"Yes," Dhang said weakly.

"You mean to say that you sought them out and offered to fight?"

"Co le—maybe."

"They came to your village and dragged you away," Andrea said. "You are as much a conscript as the peasants in the South Vietnamese Army."

"They came, too," Dhang said. He smiled. "But they missed me."

"Have you no pity for these children?" Andrea asked, working the conversation her way.

"Of course!" Dhang insisted.

"Then show me that you are a compassionate

147

young man. Bring your battalion commander here so I may talk with him."

"No!"

"*Duoc roi.* Take me to him instead," Andrea insisted.

Dhang relented. "I will go see if he will speak to you."

Nygoyen appeared again. It was obvious that he had come more out of curiosity than worry over the sick children. "You are becoming most trouble-some," he said to Andrea.

"A child has died," Andrea said. "Please help us."

Nygoyen Li's temper started to boil. "I have told you that I have no medicine!" he shouted.

Andrea yelled back, "Then let us go!"

"Impossible!" Nygoyen Li snapped out of control. "The Black Eagles are right behind—" He suddenly shut up.

Now Andrea realized that Falconi and the others were dogging their trail. She felt good, but she suppressed the desire to grin in the Viet Cong's face. Andrea also realized that there was no chance that Nygoyen Li would release anybody.

"Do not call me again or I will punish you all!" Nygoyen Li said furiously. He was angry with himself for revealing the true situation. He walked away.

Dhang stepped forward. "I have an extra shirt," he said, pulling the priceless item out of the haver-sack he wore over his shoulder.

"*Durng lai!*" came Nygoyen Li's voice. He returned, grabbing the young Viet Cong soldier and slapping his face. "You are too soft, comrade.

148

Return to your squad. I will have a more devoted soldier of socialism take your place!"

Andrea, sorry that the youngster had gotten into trouble, watched him walk forlornly away. She looked back into the expression of fury on Nygoyen Li's face.

Now Andrea knew she had to escape for sure.

CHAPTER 12

Company Commander Khung had personally assigned the ambush positions to the VC chosen to man them. He had taken his worst troops—mostly conscripted peasants who had been dragged away from their home villages—and spread them out thinly along a weak line of resistance. No serious consideration was given to a possible victory. The poor bastards were cannon-fodder, meant to soak up whatever hell the Americans could throw at them.

Several reinforced platoons of more reliable fighters were lying in wait behind them, ready to pounce on any attackers that would unwisely break through the pitifully weak front lines. Nygoyen Li, with Khung respectfully following, walked from position to position along the pseudodefensive perimeter where the second-rate VC, like sacrificial lambs, waited for the slaughter.

These young Viet Cong were highly suspicious of this honor that had been thrust upon them. Always, in the past, they had been chosen to perform the most degrading and menial of housekeeping and maintenance tasks. These were the ones who dug latrines, hauled heavy loads, and cleaned up after meals. Now, suddenly, they had been chosen to be the first to absorb an assault from the enemy. The same enemy, they knew so well, who had been kicking hell out of the crème de la crème of Khung's regular rifle platoons.

Khung, close to the battalion commander, spoke softly to him. "I am worried that many of these vermin might bolt or attempt to surrender."

Nygoyen Li, who had experienced his share of time leading reluctant troops, nodded in complete understanding. "Do you have any idea who might be the weakest?"

"Yes," Khung answered. "I pride myself in personally knowing the men in my company."

"*Duoc roi,* Comrade Company Commander," Nygoyen Li said. "Tell me who might be a particular problem as we walk the line."

The two officers began the short tour. After strolling past the first two positions, Khung slowed down, and signaled with a slight nod of his head. Nygoyen Li, taking the hint, stopped at the soldier standing there.

"*Chao ong,* Comrade Soldier," Nygoyen Li said, displaying a toothy grin.

"*Chao ong,* Comrade Battalion Commander."

"So this is where you will be killing the Americans from, eh?"

"Yes, Comrade Battalion Commander," the kid answered.

"Mmm," Nygoyen Li said. He squatted down and peered outward from the youngster's position. "You have a good field of fire. Do you see that tree over there? The one with the thick roots?"

"Yes, Comrade Battalion Commander."

"That is where you will most likely see the Americans," Nygoyen Li said. "Keep your eyes on that spot. They won't stand a chance."

"Really, Comrade Battalion Commander?"

"Toi nghi nhu vay," Nygoyen Li answered in the affirmative. "The gangsters will fall in bunches in front of you."

Encouraged, the young man grinned, then peered through the sight of his AK47 at the place indicated. "I am ready!"

Satisfied, Nygoyen Li and Khung continued the tour. They found another weakling, an older man. Undoubtedly he had a wife and children back in his home village. The Viet Cong's uneasiness was visible on his face. Nygoyen Li once more gave his best rendition of a friendly smile. *"Ong manh gioi cho?"* he asked.

"I am fine," the VC answered insincerely.

Nygoyen used the same ploy on this one. "You have a great field of fire, Comrade Soldier. The cowardly Americans will fall from your shooting."

"I do not have many bullets," the man complained.

"There are not many of them," Nygoyen Li said.

The VC squinted his eyes. "I cannot see well. I am too old to be here."

"Fight bravely tomorrow morning," Nygoyen Li assured him. "And you will return to your village and family soon."

"Duoc roi—that's good," the older man said.

Nygoyen Li and Khung walked the rest of the way to the ambush site, pausing four more times to bolster the reluctant guerrillas' fighting spirit. Finally, doing all they could, they turned toward the rear to visit the platoons situated behind the expendables.

These other units were a completely different story. Highly motivated, experienced, superbly equipped, and eager, these were the best that Khung had. These men had fought before, and the mauling they'd taken from the Black Eagles was the worst they had experienced. They wanted revenge, and Nygoyen Li was going to see they got it.

"Comrades," he said, addressing them as a group, "tomorrow's action is well designed to bring us the victory we want. After the Americans break through the line, they will be flush with false confidence and hope. Thinking they have won yet again, they will walk like pigs to a slaughter in front of your weaponry."

The eager troops shouted their approval and enthusiasm for the battle ahead.

"Di thi di! Di thi di!"

The monsoon night rolled in on the Viet Cong camp, locking it up in a rainy, cold blanket of inky darkness. The nurses and children slept fitfully, while little bodies racked by flu and fever tried to recover from the previous day's exhausting journey. Although tired and cold, the women had taken the

154

trouble to make another lean-to for the children to sleep in.

One person, however, was wide awake.

Andrea Thuy, still wearing her boots, was as alert as a hunting tigress. When she'd finally settled down after a final check of the children, she'd not removed the footgear. Now, hearing the falling rain splattering down on the palm frond roof of the shelter, she silently sat up, then got to her feet.

She paused at the door of the lean-to, peering out until she spotted where the sleepy guard leaned against a nearby tree. Using the sound of the rain as a cover, Andrea eased around the side of the structure, then moved quickly into the jungle.

Andrea's escape was a reluctant one on her part. In truth, she had left Betty Lou, Jean, and the children in great danger. The Viet Cong did not admire people who escaped their captivity. Instead, the Orientals felt as if they'd lost face. Anyone on duty or with any responsibility at all for the departing captive was severely punished—sometimes to the point of being executed. Andrea was glad that the kindly kid Dhang who had given them his precious poncho was not the guard that night.

Her mind also reflected on her companions and their little patients. No doubt Battalion Commander Nygoyen Li would take some punitive action against them. More than likely he would not permit them to build any more lean-tos in the future. It would be the same as a sentence of slow death to the kids.

But if Andrea succeeded and found Falconi, she could guide him and the Black Eagles back for a final showdown with the Viet Cong.

155

Andrea, moving slowly, continued her journey through the night. She lost track of time and distance to the point that she was surprised to note that the grayness of a monsoon dawn had lightened the jungle. Now, with even that weak light, her compass would come in handy. She ripped open the inner seam of her fatigue trousers and withdrew a small compass sewn in there. The young Eurasian also had matches, a wire saw, and a thin blade secreted on her clothing. But, under the close Viet Cong guard, she'd been unable to withdraw the items. A quick glance showed her that she'd been heading south through instinct. That was the exact direction she wished to go.

Now, still unable to see well, she pushed through the thick brush. The drops of water shaken off the leaves and branches soaked her as bad as if she'd been out in the open with the rain falling directly on her. But determination and purpose kept the cold and wet from bothering her as she fought the thick vegetation. Suddenly and unexpectedly, she broke out into an open area. It was something she hadn't expected.

And neither did the three-man Viet Cong picket post who looked at her in shock and surprise.

Gunnar Olson was the last man to toss his C-ration can into the sump. Malpractice McCorckel, overseeing the small hole serving as a garbage dump, used his entrenching tool to fill in the excavation.

The reason they carefully covered up their breakfast's remnants was not so much for sanitary purposes as it was to conceal their trail from any potential trackers. Falconi was well aware of the possibility the Viet Cong might swing around and try to hit them from the rear.

The Black Eagles silently loaded up for the day's march. They swung their jungle rucksacks up on their muscular shoulders. After shifting around a bit for a comfortable adjustment, they picked up the AK47s and were ready to move out.

Gunnar Olson, loaded down with extra box magazines, had the RPK light machine gun slung across his neck so that it hung down in front of him. The Norwegian-American didn't mind the extra weight. Heavy weaponry—as defined by the U.S. Army meaning machine guns, recoilless rifles, and mortars—were his passion. Particularly the larger, heavy caliber automatic types. He liked the feeling of extra firepower and knowing that his buddies depended on him to back them up in both the attack and defense. And there was not a Black Eagle who would deny Gunnar's artistry in rear-guard actions.

Sergeant Major Top Gordon, his face drawn with fatigue, watched the men form up. When they were all in position, he looked to Lieutenant Colonel Robert Falconi. "Sir, the detachment's all present and accounted for," he said, using the stock military phrase.

Falconi gave a little wave. "Carry on, Sergeant Major."

Top looked up at the head of the small column. "Move out, Archie."

Archie, without a word, turned and stepped out toward the north. He did his job automatically but thoroughly. He was driven on by frantic worry about Betty Lou Pemberton, the only woman he had ever loved.

Archie had been giving quite a lot of thought to that relationship. At night when he should have been sleeping, the scout mulled over the situation in his mind. It all boiled down to one solitary thing—what the hell should he do?

Betty Lou wanted him out of the Black Eagles. Archie couldn't blame her much for that. Any woman who wanted a normal home with the proverbial picket fence and kids could hardly put up with a husband who ran off into the wild hinterlands of southeast Asia for the sole purpose of killing people and destroying property. Even if it could be done on a nine-to-five basis like a regular eight-hour job, not too many women wanted their soulmates risking their necks in a very dangerous profession.

On the other hand, Archie was a Black Eagle. He'd volunteered to serve with the detachment doing what he considered an important job. It might be clandestine as hell with plenty of peril and no glory, but that was the type of fighting that Archie preferred. He was a professional soldier.

Of course he could always leave the detachment and return to the conventional side of the Army. After all his service in Vietnam, he'd end up in a peacetime garrison job. There were airborne units like the 82nd and XVIIIth Corps at Fort Bragg where he could do straight duty in a parachute rifle company. It would be fun to make a lot of parachute jumps, but on the other hand Archie could never stand the spit-and-polish of such outfits. Perhaps

Special Forces was more up his alley. There would be plenty of field exercises and the Green Berets weren't real keen on spit-shined boots and shiny brass as long as you were good in your own Military Occupational Specialty and the ones you were cross-trained in.

But Archie realized Betty Lou wouldn't go for that, either.

She flat wanted him out of the Army. If he didn't go, she'd leave him. It would break his heart, but what could he do? Finally, he decided to push all that out of his mind until later. Right now, he'd concentrate on getting her back from the Viet Cong. Then they'd decide their future together.

Suddenly Archie's complete attention jumped to another subject—the two badly concealed Viet Cong he could see a bare fifteen meters ahead of him.

He simultaneously dropped flat to the soaking ground while giving a hand-and-arm signal back to Paulo Garcia who trailed him by a few meters. Paulo, per Standing Operating Procedures, passed the silent warning on to the others. In the matter of two heartbeats, the entire detachment was lying low in wait.

Archie carefully pulled his binoculars from their case. He focused them on the Viet Cong he could see. By studying their faces, he could tell they were extremely nervous. Their eyes darted back and forth and they constantly licked at their dry lips. After replacing the field glasses, Archie crawled forward another five meters to see if he could spot more VC. His efforts were rewarded by the sight of three more positions. Satisfied, he pulled back and got to his feet when he reached a place where he was out of sight of the Reds.

Falconi saw the scout making a quick but silent approach. He waited for Archie to join him. "What's up?"

"Charlie ambush ahead, sir," Archie said. "They're strung out pretty thin. Frankly, I think we got some o' their fuckups here."

Falconi took a moment to think. "Okay. They're probably just out there to slow us down. Since we're not fooled, we'll make a straight-out attack on their positions and wipe the bastards out."

"Yes, sir," Archie agreed. He was impatient as hell to reach Betty Lou and the other women.

"Fetch Swift Elk and Top," Falconi said. "The sooner we set this thing up, the sooner we can crash through there."

Wordlessly, Archie crawled off to tend to the task.

Andrea and the trio of young VC stared at each other for a brief second.

Then she reacted.

The athletic young woman exploded into a running *jodan yoko geri* karate kick against the nearest guerrilla. Spinning quickly into positon for her second attack, Andrea delivered a devastating *mae geri* front kick into the unlucky guy's testicles. He gasped, turned blue, and slowly sank to the ground holding his pulverized crotch.

Frightened out of his wits by this feminine whirlwind of ferocity, the third Viet Cong turned in a blind panic—and ran straight into the thick trunk of a tree that had been behind him.

Andrea glanced at the three men on the ground. Two were unconscious and the third was in so much agony that he didn't give a damn about anything. She smiled thinking of the comic sight of the one who ran into the tree knocking himself silly. Methodically she picked up an AK47 assault rifle and helped herself to a couple of bandoleers of ammunition.

After another appraising look at the human wreckage she was leaving, the beautiful Eurasian woman decided against shooting them. It would make a lot of noise and would surely bring many more Viet Cong in the area down on her.

A quick check of her compass showed which way was south. She stepped out quickly in that direction, anxious to link up with Falconi and the Black Eagles.

CHAPTER 13

The Black Eagles moved forward as skirmishers, their battle line spread out along the Viet Cong main line of resistance.

Gunnar Olson, the RPK light machine gun's sling around his neck for support, expertly laid down covering fire with sporadic but expert squeezes on the trigger that hosed out firebursts of six and seven rounds.

The enemy defensive line was a dispirited one that showed little promise of developing into a serious threat. Falconi decided that the best course of action would be to smash it flat as quickly as possible.

"Move out!" he bellowed loud enough to be heard over the rain. "Charge!"

The detachment swept through the rain-drenched jungle continuing to throw out a curtain of fire ahead of it. A few panicky shots were fired back, but these more gutsy Viet Cong paid for their impetuous acts by receiving heavy volleys from the Black Eagles.

A couple of points of resistance actually pinned down Archie and Top Gordon on one occasion. But Gunnar Olson ran forward and took cover behind a fallen tree. Bracing the barrel of the machine gun on the dead trunk, he fired an entire magazine of 7.62 rounds so close to their heads that the scout's and sergeant major's ears popped from the concussion.

But the job was done, and the Black Eagles were able to advance once again. In fact, movement became so easy that their battle line was not dressed properly. Top Gordon quickly straightened things out with a few coarse expletives directed at the offending individuals.

A full five minutes passed without incident. Blue Richards and Calvin Culpepper held the left flank. Blue, keeping on the alert, spoke to his companion without shifting his eyes from potential points of attack. "Whattaya think, Calvin?"

Calvin, also staying on the alert, slowly shook his head. "I cain't make no sense out of this. Maybe them Charlies are running outta ammo and guts, man."

"Yeah," Blue answered back. "Anyhow, I think—"

An abrupt explosion of incoming rounds slapped into their area from the far left. Both men instinctively turned toward the assault and fired back. Blue was farther out than Calvin, so he was caught in a dangerous situation.

"Cover me, Calvin!" he yelled. "I gotta move back outta here."

"C'mon, my man!" Calvin responded. He shifted his fire up and toward the front. "Make your move!"

164

Blue didn't dare get to his feet. He had to push himself backward through the mud and wet. "Damn!" he complained. "I feel like a hawg in a waller!"

"Keep on a-wallering this way," Calvin said, maintaining the cover fire.

Blue finally extracted himself from immediate danger. When he joined Calvin, he quickly suggested. "Let's get on back with the others."

"That's the smartest thing I've heard in a long, long time," Calvin said. "Let's hat up!"

They both rose to a kneeling position and emptied their Ak47s at the pressing Viet Cong trying to storm their new position. The Reds ducked long enough for the pair to break loose and head in toward the center of the line.

At the same time, on the opposite end of the Black Eagle formation, Malpractice McCorckel and Paulo Garcia were having similar problems.

A strong section of Viet Cong riflemen made a flanking attack on their position. The assault was so unexpected and swift that Paulo was completely cut off. He was forced down into a small hollow in a grove of bamboo. It was an excellent defensive position, but two factors would prevent it from being a long-lasting one. Paulo would be out of ammunition after a while, and he was also strongly outnumbered by a determined enemy of elite fighters who were willing to risk their collective lives to blow him away.

Malpractice, with no way of communicating with the others, had to act fast. Damning caution, he moved forward into the withering fire that splattered through the wet vegetation. When he reached a point where he could easily see the nearest VC, the detachment medic brought up the AK47 and fired short bursts of full automatic fire.

Paulo, down in the depression, was up to his knees in cold water. Madder than hell and beginning to shiver, he quickly noted the sound of firing from his left rear. The marine knew that Malpractice had moved up to take off some of the pressure.

"Okay," he said under his breath as he slapped a fresh 30-round magazine into the communist weapon. *"Semper Fi,* you assholes!"

Paulo stuck the muzzle over the top of the hollow and fired blindly toward the Viet Cong. When he heard Malpractice join his fusillade, he quickly scrambled out of the wide hole and ran like hell until he reached his partner.

"I thought you'd never get here," Malpractice said as Paulo slid across the wet ground to join him.

"Your invitation got held up in the mail," Paulo said, turning around to renew his shooting. "Get moving."

Malpractice leaped up and bounded toward the center of the detachment. After he'd gone a few meters, he found good cover. He got behind it and began blasting toward the VC.

Paulo, like before, withdrew until he rejoined him. They continued the game, gradually breaking full contact with the enemy.

But things weren't a hell of a lot better in the center of the line.

An extremely heavy attack hit Falconi, Archie Dobbs, Top Gordon, and Ray Swift Elk. Gunnar

Olson was with their group, but had positioned himself farther back to give his machine gun more working room.

The four main men had to fire in wildly sporadic bursts as they swung the muzzles of their AK47s in wide arcs to cover all the charging Viet Cong. Falconi, pulling double-duty as a combination commanding officer/rifleman, tried to maintain tabs on the overall tactical situation while keeping the hard-pressing VC off his ass. Finally, he noted that he and his three companions were being drawn apart by the circumstances of the battle. If they lost touch, then the entire middle of the Black Eagle battle line would collapse with poor Gunnar trying to hold things together on his own.

"Move in!" Falconi yelled over the sound of the shooting. "And let's make a slow withdrawal. Go! Go!"

Archie, as usual, was the farthest out. His move back to the others was halted momentarily by a trio of determined Red guerrillas who saw a chance to cut him off and chop him up to their hearts' content.

But they hadn't reckoned on Gunnar the Gunner.

Gunnar advanced into the fighting, angling off past Top Gordon. When he got into the right position, he simply pointed the machine gun in the right direction and played a deadly tune of three ten-round bursts. The flaying bullets, packed close together, slammed into the Viet Cong with the force of artillery shrapnel. The enemy troops were thrown together, bouncing off each other before rolling to the ground. All this happened in one explosive, violent second.

167

Archie, always the man of opportunity, saw his chance and broke loose. "Thanks, Gunnar!" he yelled as he pulled in with the others.

"Ingen orsak," Gunnar replied politely in Norwegian.

The center of the line formed up just in time to meet another attack. But this more organized formation, with Gunnar's support fire closer now, swept away the front rank of the charging Viet Cong, causing those farther back to prudently hold up the effort.

Now the flankers had moved in and joined the main body. Blue Richards and Calvin Culpepper came in from the left while Malpractice McCorckel and Paulo Garcia linked up from the right side of the line.

"Ain't this a hell of a way to make a living?" Paulo asked. Although all were soaking wet from running through the dripping vegetation, Paulo was worse off from the experience in the rain-filled hollow.

"Knock off the unnecessary bullshit!" Falconi snapped. "The Charlies have backed off for a bit. It looks like a good time to hit 'em where it hurts. As skirmishers—Gunnar to the rear—move out!"

The Black Eagles advanced forward through the jungle, spread out enough to avoid being a packed target, yet close enough to have the ability to throw out a shield of heavy fire ahead of them. Gunnar, as always, moved up and down the line, waiting to see where his heavier weapon might become useful.

They met the VC in a short fifteen seconds. A terrific firefight built up. The flapping bullets from both sides cut leaves and branches off the trees and bushes with gardenerlike precision. For a few moments it was a Mexican stand-off, but the Viet Cong's strength built up rapidly as other platoons moved in as reinforcements. Again, Falconi made a quick reading of the tactical situation.

"Pull back! Go! Go!"

The Black Eagles quickly broke contact. They were able to pull back out of harm's way due to the goosey attitude of the Charlies, who had been taking quite a mauling since the battle began.

After withdrawing twenty meters, Falconi halted his men and formed them up for another expected enemy charge.

There was hardly a heartbeat before the Viet Cong launched their attack. Obviously buoyed up by their officer and NCOs, the guerrillas came on in a rush, yelling loudly. As usual, pushed by their buddies in the rear, the front ranks were sacrificed. But this time, the second line of Charlies also caught unmitigated hellfire.

The Black Eagles, concealed among a stand of fallen trees, were in both high and low positions. It was not unlike the close-packed defensive fire of earlier centuries when one rank of men knelt in front and the second rank, standing, fired over the heads to deliver a combined volley of devastation and death.

Falconi's men madly fired countless fusillades, pausing only when it was necessary to insert fresh magazines of ammo. The endless explosive din of sustained fire punished eardrums on both sides. Gunnar, resting his weapon in the fork of a tree, barely had to aim as he swung the weapon back and forth along the length of the battle line.

Company Commander Khung saw this as a chance to finally crush the tenacious pursuers who had been chopping his men to bits. Screaming in uncontrolled fury, he urged his men forward into the blasting hell that Falconi's men were dishing out.

But motivation is a vital key to victory, and the situation of the three women in the Reds' hands was foremost in the mind of every Black Eagle. They stepped up their defensive fire until the Viet Cong front line, which began as its fourth line, melted down into bloody heaps on the jungle ground. The Charlies farther back began a spontaneous withdrawal that their section leaders could not stem even with punches and kicks.

"After 'em!" Falconi yelled. "Go! Go!"

Once more the detachment counterattacked. They met no resistance as they swept forward. It looked like an easy victory from that point on, but Falconi suddenly shouted, "Hold up! Cease fire! Let's get back! Go!"

Well-trained soldiers ask no questions of orders. Although puzzled by this sudden abandonment of what seemed an easy victory, the Black Eagles instantly obeyed. As before, contact with the enemy was broken, and they headed for the rear.

Falconi led them past the fallen trees where defense had been so good, until he reached an area they had traveled through earlier. The lieutenant colonel didn't waste an instant as he personally assigned fighting positions to each man.

Archie Dobbs, settling behind the palm bush chosen for him, glanced around. "Damn, sir! This

170

looks like we're setting up an old-fashioned ambush."

"Give the man a cigar," Falconi said while pointing out a place for Gunnar's machine gun. "That's exactly what we're doing!"

An unreal silence now prevailed through the thick vegetation. Only the constant spattering of rain on leaves could be heard. The Black Eagles settled down in almost lethargic reveries until a rumble of distant thunder brought their mental processes back to the present dangers they faced.

A full half hour passed before a pair of Viet Cong crept into the area. The two point men for the main body moved slowly and warily. They saw nothing of the nine men who were concealed a short distance from the trail they followed.

Another five minutes passed before the larger group of Charlies appeared. They were in a double-column formation. If the terrain had been more wide open they would have been formed into a better arrangement that gave good all-around protection. But in the confines of the jungle, that was the best they could do.

And that was fine with Falconi.

He stood up and raked the entire Viet Cong unit with a full magazine from his AK47. The other Black Eagles followed suit, massacring the men charging toward the front of their weapons. The surviving Charlies broke and ran.

Now the Black Eagles followed up their success by charging after the fleeing enemy. Isolated groups of two and three VC tried to turn and fire, but they were shot down and swept over by Falconi's

171

determined men.

But the Red officers soon regained control of their men, forming up in close-packed fire-and-maneuver teams that began to slow down the pursuit, permitting them a more dignified retreat. The initial squads paid a bitter price as they were cut down, but more joined in the tactic until Falconi was forced to call off the chase.

Top Gordon gathered up the men and brought them all into the commander's immediate area. "We won the battle but not the war," Falconi reminded them. "There're still three women relying on us to bring them back out of this hell. Let's get more ammo off the dead Charlies and head back to this war. It's far from over."

Tired but determined, the men turned to the task of resupply. Archie Dobbs properly summed up the situation when he made an offhand remark to Malpractice McCorckel:

"This looks like it's going to be a long, tough, fucking operation."

Malpractice nodded. "Remember what the Old Man always says."

"Yeah," Archie replied. "Nobody said this job was going to be easy."

CHAPTER 14

The North Vietnamese Army District Headquarters at Ben Quang consisted of a ramshackle frame building located close to the center of the small city. The place was an eyesore as well as a firetrap. The only bright part of the structure was a colorful red-and-gold sign which identified it as:

LUC-QUAN
CONG HOA XA HOI CHU NGHIA
VIET-NAM

Sogolov noticed it as the Soviet command car pulled up in front of the rickety edifice. Before the KGB man could ask, General Truong Van translated for him. "It says," Truong remarked, "Army of the Socialist Republic of Vietnam."

"Shouldn't that say North Vietnam?" Sogolov inquired.

Truong shook his head. "Since we do not recognize the sovereignty of South Vietnam, why would we refer to ourselves in any other manner than what the sign implies?"

"You are correct, of course, Comrade General," Sogolov said.

The driver turned off the car's engine. He immediately got out and opened the door for the two officers. He stood at attention, waiting until they entered the building before he relaxed and closed up the car once again. Then, glad to be away from the subtle bickering of his passengers, he got into the front seat to enjoy a nap until they returned.

Sogolov and Truong were expected by the staff inside. They marched past a saluting guard at the front door to be met by a severe and proper captain. He also saluted and issued a polite, respectful greeting. Gesturing for them to follow him, he escorted them up to the second floor where the district military intelligence office was located. Once there, they were served the obligatory hot coffee before the major in charge of the bureau made his appearance.

He was a short, stocky man with a bald head. The manila folder under his arm gave good indication that he hadn't come to make small talk. "I have information, comrades," he announced without ceremony. "It has only lately arrived and has been decoded."

"I trust it is important," Truong said coldly. "That would be a good reason for this lack of proper protocol."

"I am sorry, Comrade General and Comrade Colonel," the major said. "I am Major Dnai."

"We are pleased to meet you, Comrade Major,"

Truong said. *"Parlez-vous français?* The comrade Russian does not speak our language."

"Ah! *Pardonnez-moi, s'il vous plaît.* I did not realize it," Dnai said in French.

"Please give us the latest intelligence you have received," Sogolov said impatiently.

"Mais oui, Camarade Colonel," Major Dnai said. "The first bit of information is most unfortunate. The key prisoner has escaped."

Sogolov's face turned scarlet with rage. *"Quel dommage!* When did this happen?"

"A couple of nights ago," Dnai answered. "Her departure was discovered in the morning. The guard on duty stated that he did not hear or see anything unusual during the night."

Sogolov, so angry he almost spat on the floor, spoke through clenched teeth. "I hope the sentry was properly disciplined."

"He was shot, Comrade Colonel," the major said in a matter-of-fact tone. "But, no matter, for the woman we are positive is Andrea Thuy is gone."

Truong felt his nation and race's prestige was about to come under severe criticism. "The comrades in the Viet Cong are guerrillas, Comrade Colonel. They are not as sophisticated or well trained as the North Vietnamese regulars."

Sogolov was now surprisingly cool. "Of course not, Comrade General. We must take that into consideration." He looked back at Dnai. "Any more news?"

"None good, I fear, Comrade Colonel," the major said. "Comrade Battalion Commander Nygoyen Li's best company has almost been completely wiped

175

out by Falconi's Black Eagles."

"That man and his unit must be destroyed!" Sogolov exclaimed.

"As you know," Truong said, "a KGB man has already tried."

Sogolov chose to ignore the veiled insult. "What about the NVA battalion that I have requested?"

"It should be close to the operational area now, Comrade Colonel," the major said.

"Contact the commander and tell him to speed up the march," Sogolov said, getting to his feet. "We will rendezvous with him at the agreed coordinates in the northern portion of the province." He snapped his fingers at Truong. *"Venez!* Come! We must hurry away."

Infuriated by the Russian's casual and insulting manner, Truong nevertheless dutifully followed him.

Betty Lou Pemberton's ears rang for several long seconds after Company Commander Khung's series of hard slaps to her face. He spoke to her in harsh broken English:

"How you help your friend escape?" he asked.

"I didn't!" Betty Lou cried. She was angry and hateful toward Andrea for fleeing and leaving her and Jean alone with the children. "She didn't say anything to me about escape plans."

"What is her name?" Khung asked.

Betty Lou, coached long before they had even gone to Nui Dep about Andrea's special circumstances, bravely replied, "She is called Dow."

Khung hit her again. "What is her name?"

Betty Lou sobbed. "I told you!"

Khung, his face distorted with hot anger, took the opportunity to punch her hard with his closed fist.

Betty Lou cried out in pain as she was knocked to the wet ground. "Please! Please!"

Nugent, Nygoyen Li's intelligence officer, stepped into the scene. "Wait, Comrade Company Commander!"

Khung spun and faced him. "What is it you say to me?"

"I am the official interrogator in this unit," Nugent insisted. "You have no right to question the prisoner."

"You have done no good with her," Khung said. "So I have taken over."

"That does not matter," Nugent said. "You are far too cruel with her. Go away."

"I will speak to the comrade battalion commander," Khung said, stalking away in anger.

Nugent knelt and helped Betty Lou to her feet. "You must answer questions," he said. "If you do not give me information, then Khung will return and be even more cruel to you."

Betty Lou, emotionally drained and upset, could do no more than sob.

"You know what he do with you?" Nugent asked. "He give you to men for lots of fuck. You want that?"

Betty Lou was incapable of clear thinking. The previous days of worrying and caring for the children under the circumstances of a forced march through the driving rain had left her incapable of clear, logical thinking. If she'd been able to think clearly, she would have noted the fact that the two Viet Cong had spoken in English to each other for her benefit. If Betty Lou had training as an intelligence agent, she would also have recognized that the pair of VC officers were playing "Mutt-and-Jeff" interrogation. This was where one was cruel and demanding while the other showed compassion and understanding, wanting answers only to end the prisoner's torment.

"Please," Nugent said, continuing the role. "Let me help you, Miss Nurse. Answer the question. What is friend's name?"

"Oh, God!" Betty Lou sobbed. "Andrea—Andrea Thuy!"

The North Vietnamese reinforced rifle company was made up of well-equipped veterans. Their field gear was of the latest Red Chinese model and even included steel helmets. While motor transport did not exist for them, at least the signals section was supplied with the most up-to-date versions of the Soviet R-series communication equipment.

The unit's commander, a tough individual named Giang, had the right to feel absolutely confident that his men could carry out any mission assigned them even in heavy monsoon weather. But even an elite NVA rifle unit had to rest sometime, so he had called a halt for the day as the evening quickly turned into almost total darkness.

The soldiers, capable and expert in jungle living

and fighting, had built small, hot fires despite the rain. They boiled their rice and heated their tea after a long hard day of rapid marching. Captain Giang, looking out at the cookfires from beneath his poncho-covered command post, sipped his own tea and contemplated the situation with his adjutant.

Their soft, muted conversation was interrupted by the arrival of the signal sergeant. "I have a message for you, Comrade Captain," he announced with a salute.

Giang took the piece of paper and carefully read it. Although not a well-educated man, he had a sharp wit and deep intellect. "Ah! It is confirmation that one of the nurses caught by the Viet Cong comrade was indeed the notorious woman criminal Andrea Thuy."

The adjutant, a sour old campaigner, was not readily impressed by anything much. "How do they know this?" he asked in a sour tone.

"Another of the nurses confessed," Giang answered.

The adjutant shrugged. "So? She was probably beaten or raped. She would say anything they wanted."

"They only wanted this information if it were the truth," Giang said. "There was nothing to be gained by a coerced statement involving a known war criminal."

The adjutant was satisfied. "Then our Viet Cong comrades have done quite well."

"Yes," Giang said, displaying a wide grin. "But she escaped from them."

Now the adjutant laughed. "Ah, our well-motivated but inept brothers. Damned bunch of rice farmers!"

Giang fetched his map case and brought out the topographical sheet on the operational area. After studying the document for several long minutes, he folded it up and returned it to the canvas container. "The woman could not have chosen a worse place from which to escape," he said. "She must pass through our area in order to go south. If she tried a roundabout route, she would spend days in travel, then stumble into Laos on the one hand, or the South China sea on the other."

"You sound as if you think we will be recapturing her ourselves," the other officer remarked.

"Of course," Giang said. "Study your map and you will agree. It is only a matter of hours before we have her in our own prisoner of war cage."

Dhang, the young VC who had shown so much compassion toward the nurses and children, was close to tears. Since Andrea Thuy's escape, he had been reassigned as their guard. His affection for the noncombatants had not abated a bit during his short absence from them.

"Please!" he begged Jean. "You must cooperate fully with the comrade battalion commander."

Jean, who had been asked to back up Betty Lou's claim that the escaped woman was Andrea Thuy, had refused to talk. She'd been subjected to Mutt-and-Jeff and given a rough beating which included several hard kicks. But she had refused to divulge any information other than her name.

Jean, one eye blackened and swollen shut, clutched her sore ribs. "Do not give me advice, Dhang," she whispered through bloody lips. "If you continue, I will no longer trust you or be your friend."

"But, Xinh!" he insisted, using her proper Vietnamese name. "You do not realize the peril you are in."

"I understand it well," Jean said. She glanced toward the lean-to where Betty Lou huddled with the children. "Poor girl! She is lost out here in this filthy war. It would have been better if she'd stayed back at Long Binh to care for wounded soldiers."

"Do not worry about her!" Dhang begged. "Tell them the truth and beg forgiveness. Show that you are repentant and sorry for betraying the people's struggle for freedom, Xinh. If you do so they will not shoot you."

Xinh looked up at him, her uninjured eye opened wide in surprise. "Are you saying they are going to execute me, Dhang?"

"Yes," Dhang said. "Nygoyen Li must do so to save face."

Jean nodded, knowing he was telling the truth. She accepted her fate with the philosophical resignation of the Orient. "It would seem," she said softly, "that it is my karma to die out here in this diabolical rain. *Phai!*"

CHAPTER 15

Betty Lou and Jean McCorckel made another nervous check of the sick kids. Both women fought back sobs as they sought to comfort the little ones in their care. The pair smiled and spoke to their charges in soft, comforting voices.

Three more of the toddlers were close to death. Their shallow, gurgling breath was a sure sign of pneumonia.

"God!" Betty Lou said. "If we only had some penicillin."

"There is nothing," Jean said. "All we can do is give them our love and hope that will comfort their tiny hearts."

"Dhang was so kind to give us his poncho," Betty Lou said. "At least that keeps the kids from having direct contact with the wet ground." She tenderly stroked the forehead of the child who seemed the worst. His skin was hot and dry as the fever inside him raged unchecked. His tiny lungs, filled with fluid, could only work in quick pants. "Poor baby," she cooed. The American nurse looked up at her friend. "I'm sorry, Jean."

"About what?"

"For telling them who Andrea really was," Betty Lou said. "If I'd kept my mouth shut they wouldn't have known."

Jean was more knowledgeable of such situations. "Then they would have continued the interrogation until you would not have known whether to deny or confirm her true identity."

"They questioned you," Betty Lou said. "But you did not betray Andrea."

"Let us not dwell on it," Jean said. "You are a good friend to both Andrea and me, Betty Lou. I shall always love you as a sister."

"And I you, Jean!"

They embraced, holding each other tight. Jean had not told Betty Lou of the threat of execution. There was nothing to be gained by adding this worry to the problems they faced. If the Viet Cong decided to shoot her, they would do it. If, by some wild stretch of luck, their decision was to let her alone, then nothing would be gained by increasing Betty Lou's anxiety.

"Do we have any rice left?" Betty Lou asked.

"A bit," Jean answered. "Is it time to feed the children?"

"It would be a good idea," Betty Lou said. The two nurses, their rations seriously reduced as a punishment since Andrea's escape, still managed to set aside enough of their meager food to give a little extra to the children. They needed all the extra nourishment their little bodies could get in order to fight off the flu and pneumonia that grew worse each day.

The two nurses had saved up the day's issue and kept it rolled up in a large *rung* leaf. Jean carefully opened it, and they went from child to child, giving each a small mouthful of the food. They woke up a couple who were sleeping. Although they needed their rest, they also had a dire requirement for extra nourishment.

The pitiful meal had just finished when Dhang approached them from his guard post a scant five meters away. "Xinh!" he whispered in alarm. "Here comes the comrade battalion commander and a squad of men. *"Can-than!"*

Betty Lou was puzzled. "What is he talking about?"

Jean smiled and patted her arm. "Do not worry, friend Betty Lou. The only thing that is happening, is the fulfillment of my karma."

Betty Lou had been around enough Orientals by that time to be able to fully comprehend the awful weight of that simple phrase. "Jean!"

Dhang stepped back as Nygoyen Li, Nugent, and four Viet Cong riflemen walked up to the lean-to. "Nurse Xinh!" Nugent called out sharply.

"Yes?" she answered, stepping out from the palm frond cover.

"Our intelligence service send us information about you," Nugent said in English.

Now Betty Lou was really alarmed and angry. Nugent Li was obviously speaking for her benefit. She joined her friend. "What the hell is going on?"

One of the VC roughly grabbed her and pushed

her away. *"Di di!"* he scolded her.

"You are marry with American," Nugent said.

"Yes," Jean said calmly.

"He is Black Eagle, *khong co?"*

Now Jean displayed a defiant smile. "He is Black Eagle, *cò!"*

"Because you are traitor and liar," Nugent announced, "the People's Court say you die now."

Betty Lou was staggered with shock. "What? What?"

Jean turned to Betty Lou. "Goodbye, my friend. I shall pray that we meet in the next life." Suddenly her eyes filled with tears, and her lip trembled. "Tell Malcomb I love him with all my heart, Betty Lou! Please! Tell him!"

Betty Lou charged forward and grabbed Jean, pulling her back. "No! No! No!"

One of the VC jumped between them, tearing them apart. "Do not do that, bad American person," he scolded her in his best English.

Jean now was amazingly serene. "I wish to die with dignity, Betty Lou. Goodbye, dear. Don't forget what to say to Malcomb."

"I won't," Betty Lou tearfully promised as she watched them drag her friend away.

Andrea stopped her slow foot journey long enough to make another compass check. Due to the low clouds and thick jungle flora, she was unable to shoot azimuths of any great distance. It had become necessary to walk with the navigational instrument in one hand while she constantly checked the direction in which the needle pointed.

Now, with the latest realignment of her line of travel, Andrea once again stepped out on her arduous southern trek. After a few meters, she had to look at the compass once again. When she raised her eyes, she saw the North Vietnamese Army trooper ahead. Luckily, he was looking the other way. Andrea turned to retrace her steps, and saw another.

This one also spotted her.

Andrea had no choice. She whipped up the AK47 for one brief sight picture before firing. The young woman barely had time to note the Viet Cong collapse. She had to whirl and shoot at the other since he would have heard the shot. That one died with an expression of wonderment and surprise on his face.

There was no time to waste. Andrea ran off at an oblique angle to her original direction of travel. But she'd managed to go no more than ten meters when an NVA squad appeared across her path. Slipping the weapon's selector to full-automatic, she hosed out a stream of a dozen bullets. The two most forward of the North Vietnamese pitched unceremoniously to the ground, but their buddies returned fire.

Andrea instinctively blinked and ducked as the slugs whacked the air around her. But she stood firm, firing calmly now with shorter pulls on the trigger. Her efforts produced a small pile of bodies.

The last round of the magazine had been fired. Andrea ran like hell through the slippery wet of the monsoon jungle while she inserted a fresh, full one.

More shots abruptly sounded from her left. A large tree to the right was splintered by the bullets. She returned fire and was rewarded with the sound of a scream. But Andrea had no time for gloating or self-congratulations. She had to keep moving.

More NVA appeared. They began measured volleys of semiautomatic fire. Andrea had no choice but to turn from them. Once more she came into contact with North Vietnamese. She emptied another magazine at them, forcing them back out of sight. Andrea would have liked to conserve her ammunition, but the circumstances demanded immediate response with plenty of firepower.

Her last magazine went into the weapon as she ran as fast as she could. The vegetation grew steadily thicker until she could barely move. A few meters more and she was forced to stop. A wall of brush and tangled vines rose ahead of her. Then she realized that the positioning of the Reds had not been haphazard. They had forced her into the direction they wanted. Now she was stuck in a box canyon.

For a warrior woman like Andrea, there was but one choice in the situation—death!

She knelt to meet the charge that was sure to come. Ahead, sloshing around through the wet, the NVA soldiers were making no attempt at noise discipline. It was as if they wished to announce their presence. Andrea raised the rifle to take aim at the point she expected the first to appear. But she never held the posture long.

The two men struck her from the side, simultaneously knocking her down and grabbing her weapon from her grasp. They were heavily camouflaged with branches, leaves, and camo face paint. One smiled coldly at her. *"Chao Dai Uy* Andrea Thuy," he said. "We have been expecting you."

Andrea literally growled in rage. She started to strike out, but other men had appeared and she was physically taken into custody and tied up with field telephone wire.

An officer now appeared on the scene. "Well, Andrea Thuy," he said with a smile. "It seems you are back in communist captivity again. We welcome your return to our tender mercies."

Andrea spat in his face.

The officer struck her hard, bloodying her nose with the blow. "Your troubles, dear Miss Thuy, have just begun." He motioned to his troops. "Quickly! We must rejoin the others and link up with the Viet Cong comrades. *Mau len!"*

Betty Lou squatted under the lean-to, her hands clasped tightly over her ears. She didn't want to hear the sound of the firing squad's rifles when they executed Jean.

A long time passed with no noise. Finally one of the children began crying. Betty Lou got up and tended to the child as best she could. It took nearly a quarter of an hour before the small patient went back to sleep. Betty Lou, red-eyed and exhausted, looked out the lean-to toward the Viet Cong camp.

She suddenly emitted a small cry of joy.

The firing squad, with Jean in front, were walking back toward the lean-to. The young VC Dhang came running up. "They are going to spare her!" he quickly informed Betty Lou. Then he quickly went back to his guard post.

Battalion Commander Nygoyen Li himself appeared from the crowd of people. "Greetings, American Nurse," he said to Betty Lou. "The benevolent Viet Cong and their gallant comrades in the north have shown mercy on your friend in spite of her traitorous criminal acts against the peasants and workers."

Betty Lou felt like smirking at the ridiculous remark, but she was so overjoyed at seeing Jean safe and sound that she didn't want to do anything to spoil it.

Jean was allowed to run forward. She embraced Betty Lou, holding her close. "Oh, Betty Lou! They are giving us medicine and blankets."

"What?" Betty Lou was dumbfounded by the wonderful news.

"It is true," Nygoyen Li said. "The compassionate and humane government of the People's Republic of Viet Nam has sent medical supplies down to you from Ben Quang."

"Thank you," Jean said. She nudged Betty Lou as a hint.

Betty Lou, quickly taking her cue, also showed gratitude. "Thank you for this kindness."

Nygoyen Li snapped his fingers and four of his men appeared with cardboard boxes wrapped in clear plastic. They set them in front of the lean-to. "Now," the battalion commander said. "Use these items to save the lives of the children fathered by the enemies of the people."

"Yes! Yes! Thank you!" Betty Lou said. She

forced open one of the boxes. Syringes and vials of penicillin were neatly packed on top of blankets.

The two nurses went to work. First a thick layer of blankets was put down on Dhang's poncho, then the children were arranged on it. More blankets were used to cover them. The dry warmth was greeted with soft coos and sighs from the sick children.

"Now the shots," Betty Lou said. "We mustn't waste time."

"Of course," Jean said. They began preparing to administer the antibiotic. Jean leaned forward and spoke under her breath. "A large unit of North Vietnamese infantry arrived with these supplies," she said. "They had Andrea with them."

"She was recaptured then?"

"Yes."

Betty Lou glanced up to make sure they couldn't be overheard. "Isn't it amazing that a big outfit was necessary to capture one woman?"

But Jean saw no humor in the situation. "They are among the best the NVA has," she said ominously. "And their next target is the Black Eagles."

"Robert Falconi and the others will defeat them," Betty Lou said defiantly.

"Oh, Betty Lou," Jean cautioned her. "The North Vietnamese are superbly equipped and outnumber our men twenty to one."

"I won't think about that," Betty Lou said, shaking her head. "Let's concentrate on the children."

The two nurses went back to their task.

CHAPTER 16

General Truong Van smoked slowly as the small Russian military car traveled south of Ben Quang toward the active war zone. The more distance they traveled from the city, the more the highway deteriorated. From concrete they went to macadam, then to a narrow planked road where they were forced to reduce their speed to twenty-five kilometers an hour. This final portion was maintained through the continuous, backbreaking effort of coolie labor.

At one point they were forced to come to a complete stop while a hundred young men and women worked frantically to repair a portion of the rustic thoroughfare that had been washed away by the previous night's heavy rains.

Truong's Russian companion, KGB Colonel Dimitri Sogolov, leaned forward to peer through the windshield to see what was holding them up. "Amazing! You people have so many helping hands doing work that would normally be performed by machines in other countries."

"We are a poor nation," Truong explained.

Sogolov smiled. "Your Russian big brothers will help you out. Were not the medical supplies I ordered sent to the sick children in the Viet Cong camp from the Soviet Union?"

"Yes," Truong said. Then he admitted, "It was a great propaganda coup. When the world is informed of the sick children rescued by Viet Cong hero Nygoyen Li, they will see that proper medical care was provided them."

"Another example of Russian generosity," Sogolov said.

"Yes," Truong said. "Of course there are always certain strings attached."

"What do you mean?" Sogolov demanded. He was growing weary of the other's constant and subtle complaining.

"Only that you handle such material as you see fit," Truong said. "I am a general in the North Vietnamese Army, yet I could not order the medical items out of a warehouse with the same ease that you did."

"It is a matter of procedure, protocol, and prior arrangement," Sogolov said sullenly. The KGB officer hated being put on the defensive. He settled back as the car again renewed its slow journey.

Their destination was a military outpost. Although far from the fighting, it was constructed as if it were exposed to imminent attack. The reason for this was to provide visiting VIPs from Iron Curtain countries a chance to see the front lines without actually being there. But Truong had chosen this to be their own advanced command post because of its convenient location.

Their arrival caused a scurry of ceremonious activity. The outpost commander presented himself with a small honor guard to receive the visitors. But General Truong was in no mood for parade ground nonsense.

"Take us to your headquarters bunker and give us a full briefing," he abruptly ordered. "And do so in French for the comrade colonel's consideration."

"Yes, Comrade General!" the commander quickly responded.

Truong and Sogolov were taken down to a communication trench that led past a series of pseudodefensive positions. They were taken inside and made comfortable on the plush furniture. Hot coffee was served.

"Comrade General and Comrade Colonel," the outpost commander began. "I have good news. The escaped prisoner has been recaptured by troops of the glorious people's army of North Vietnam. She is now back in custody in the camp of the Viet Cong comrades."

"Excellent!" Sogolov exclaimed. "She is too valuable to be allowed back to her own lines."

"Yes," Truong said with a slight smile. "We slant-eyed yokels manage to put things right now and then."

"So I have noticed," Sogolov said coolly.

"Also, the tactical situation is progressing nicely," the NVA officer said, continuing his briefing. "The reinforced rifle company will draw the Black Eagle gangsters into an ambush net by leading them along through a series of bogus picket and ambush points. The comrades manning these are excellent combat troops. They know how to strike back convincingly, yet break contact and flee in what the capitalist gangsters should perceive as retreats."

"Fine," Sogolov said. "Now I think the most important thing is to get the prisoner Andrea Thuy back here. I want some of your best troops dispatched to fetch her. In the meantime, contact the North Vietnamese who are with the Viet Cong comrades and have their commander give the woman a preliminary field interrogation. But no rough stuff! I will follow up here, then we will take her back to Hanoi for a full examination."

"Oui, Camarade Colonel!"

Sogolov turned to Truong. "It would appear that this situation with the Black Eagles will be wrapped up quite nicely."

"Yes," Truong agreed. "And quickly, too."

Top Gordon crawled through the tall grass, getting as soaked as if he were standing under a waterfall. He went to each man in the detachment. They were strung out in a loose skirmish line after being hastily formed up in obedience to Lieutenant Colonel Robert Falconi's order.

As Top stopped to speak to the individual Black Eagles, his message was the same:

"There's a small NVA unit ahead. Probably some sort of a picket or observation post. Archie spotted 'em and said we could mop 'em up without a lot of hassle. Wait for the word to advance."

It took him fifteen minutes to accomplish the task before he was able to return to the detachment commander. When he rejoined Falconi and Archie, the sergeant major signaled the unit's readiness with a nod.

"Okay," Falconi said. "Let's move 'em out." He emitted a quick, sharp whistle.

The entire detachment rose up and began a slow, deliberate walk forward, their weapons ready for the coming confrontation. After five minutes, Falconi caught sight of an NVA trooper. His initial shot heralded the beginning of the battle.

Archie went into action quickly, moving off to the left under the enemy's initial incoming fire. He pivoted inward and dropped behind the gnarled roots of a large jungle tree. Bringing up his AK47, he began quickly firing to lay down a base of fire for Top Gordon.

The sergeant major advanced quickly into the fight. He pumped a spray of slugs outward, hitting one NVA. Two more made an appearance and cut loose with carefully aimed salvos. Top dropped down, but the North Vietnamese did not follow up their advantage. They simply pulled back.

At the same time Calvin Culpepper and Blue Richards made contact on their side of the line. There was a brief exchange of shots as both Black Eagles and the enemy tried to reposition themselves to advantage. Ricochets zinged through the wet atmosphere blowing pieces of sodden bark off trees as the two groups of fighters tried to kill each other.

Finally, well situated, Calvin and Blue made a coordinated movement toward the enemy. Firing and maneuvering, they went forward at a rapid rate, but the Red infantrymen showed no inclination to fight. They simply disappeared back into the jungle.

"What the hell's the matter with them?" Calvin asked.

Blue shook his head. "Them boys just didn't want to tangle with us today, you ol' Buffalo Soljer."

Calvin laughed. "Yo're so ugly, you prob'ly scared 'em half to death."

"No way!" Blue protested good-naturedly. "They seen what a handsome feller I am, so they ran home to hide their wives."

Things weren't quite so humorous on the opposite side of the Black Eagle line. Paulo and Malpractice were surprised by a light flanking attack. They managed to respond, but it was difficult and took some time. The NVA did not press their advantage, however. After exchanging some more shots, they disappeared.

"I think we won that one," Paulo said, looking around puzzled.

"I don't know," Malpractice mused. "But, on the other hand, we didn't lose, neither."

Things were just as confused where the two-man fire support crew of Ray Swift Elk and Gunnar the Gunner Olson operated in the middle. They had gone forward to lend a hand if things got hairy on some part of the line. The center suddenly grew quiet, but fighting built up to the left. The two moved toward it, but suddenly things became silent there.

"What're we doing?" Gunnar asked. "Dancing with them sons of bitches?"

"They're flitting around like rabbits," Swift Elk observed.

But an abrupt burst of firing broke out to the right. They double-timed toward the action, but by the time they arrived there, things had quieted down.

"Let's find the old man," Swift Elk said.

The pair went forward until they linked up with Falconi, Top, and Archie. Archie was loudly complaining. "We can't maintain contact with 'em, sir. They shoot and run—shoot and run."

"Yeah," Falconi agreed. "From all appearances, I think we hit a small patrol. They were probably surprised as hell and just wanted to get the hell out of here." He nodded to Top. "Let's bring the guys in and get on with this pursuit."

Archie pulled the cocking handle on the AK47. "I'll lead on then, sir."

Within one minute, the detachment was back in pursuit.

Andrea Thuy, sitting on the wet ground, leaned up against a tree. Although heartsick over being recaptured, she kept her composure calm and under complete control. She was almost amused to the point of laughing by the half dozen guards who stood watch over her.

An NVA officer coming out of the thick brush nearby walked up to her. He gazed down at the woman for a long time before he spoke. *"Chao, Dai Uy Thuy,"* he said to her.

"My name is Dow," she said, knowing he did not believe her. "At any rate, have no fear. If I become

199

threatening or violent, these brave soldiers will protect you."

The officer laughed. "We are more concerned about you harming yourself, Captain Thuy," he said.

"How thoughtful!" she said scornfully.

"My name is Company Commander Giang," he said, introducing himself. "I am the senior officer of the reinforced unit that is going to destroy Falconi and his gangsters."

"Who?"

Giang ignored the role she insisted on playing. "He is walking into a trap. We are baiting it with small teams of fighters who will lead him into a large ambush we have set up for him."

Andrea's composure stayed cool though she realized that Falconi and the others faced real danger. If they were still under the impression that they faced weak, uncoordinated units, they would surely be drawn into an inescapable situation that could lead to their deaths or capture.

"I thought you might be interested to know that medicine and blankets have been provided for the sick children," Giang said, trying to set a friendly tone.

"That is most kind." Andrea knew if such a thing had happened, it would be only as part of a larger propaganda scheme to show the outside world. But she didn't want to do anything to jeopardize helping her friends and their small patients.

"I will be back later to talk to you," Giang said. "Perhaps you will have realized the advantages of cooperating with the people's army by then."

In a pig's ass, Andrea's mind spoke. But she remained outwardly calm.

Giang left her and went back to the command post. His adjutant had been waiting impatiently for him. "Comrade Company Commander, we have made contact with the Black Eagle gangsters. The Third Platoon engaged them, then broke contact and withdrew. The Americans have followed as we suspected they would."

"Duoc roi!" Giang exclaimed.

Nygoyen Li, now out of the spotlight, was nevertheless glad to hear the Black Eagles were falling into the trap being set for them. *"Murng ong!"* he called out. He started to add to the congratulations, but his officer Nugent suddenly walked up in an agitated manner. He could tell something was wrong. *"Co gi la khong?"* he asked.

"A man has deserted," Nugent reported.

"Which one?" Nygoyen Li demanded to know.

"One of the conscripts," Nugent answered. "The one named Dhang. Do you remember him, Comrade Battalion Commander? He gave his poncho to the American nurses."

CHAPTER 17

The children being cared for by Betty Lou Pemberton and Jean McCorckel had responded well and quickly to the medicine administered to them. Born in primitive surroundings, they would have perished before the third month of their lives if they had been physical weaklings. Being naturally hardy, they had already survived poor sanitation, malnourishment, and the physical dangers of the jungle environment. These biological strengths, combined with modern antibiotics, resulted in splended, rapid recovery.

Now, happy and warm under blankets, they rested and slept while the ravages of flu and pneumonia in their small bodies were being healed by the properties of up-to-date chemical technology.

Betty Lou and Jean McCorckel made a final check of their patients. They tucked in several whose restless sleep had caused them to toss and turn. A half dozen, now feeling much better, had to be given a somewhat stern lecture to settle down and not bother their sleepy neighbors.

Betty laughed about that. "It's a sure sign they are getting better," she remarked.

"Yes," Jean agreed. "A misbehaving child is a healthy child."

They went outside the lean-to to a special area that had been set up for them. Whoever wanted the children to appear healthy and happy in the propaganda program also wanted the nurses to have a better appearance. In order to make them more comfortable, a two-man pup tent had been provided, as well as a small cookstove. With increased rations, more rest, and the lessening of stress from worrying about the children, Betty Lou and Jean's demeanor had improved a great deal.

A pot of water boiled on the stove. Betty Lou, using C-rations provided by the Viet Cong, prepared cups of coffee. She gave one to Jean and they settled on the canvas camp chairs beside the small tent.

Jean, speaking low, leaned toward Betty Lou. "I hadn't the chance to tell you before, but I hear the Charlies talking. Andrea is back in camp. She is over at the command post."

"They caught her? Oh dear!" Betty Lou exclaimed.

"I don't know if we are supposed to be aware that she is here," Jean said.

"What difference would it possibly make?" Betty Lou asked. "Let's see if we can visit her."

Jean nodded. She called over to the VC guard standing a few meters away. *"Di ra,* please."

The man, openly surly, sauntered over. "What is it?" He resented the fact that their bivouac facilities were better than his own and those of his comrades.

204

"We wish to visit with our friend," Jean said. "We have heard she is with your commander."

"You cannot see her," the guard said. "It is forbidden."

Jean translated for Betty Lou. The American nurse was insistent. "Tell him we wish to speak with our friend Dhang."

Jean turned to the Charlie. *"Dau* Dhang?" she asked.

"The traitor has deserted," the guard said.

"He has run away?"

"Like a whipped dog," the guard said. He spat to show his contempt. A flurry of activity caught his attention. The VC left the nurses to see what was happening. In a few moments he returned. "A detachment of North Vietnamese has arrived," he told the nurses. "They have come to take your friend away." Without further explanation, he returned to his guard post.

"Poor Andrea!" Betty Lou exclaimed.

"Yes," Jean said. "But at least our friend Dhang has escaped these awful people."

"I wish him well," Betty Lou said. "I shall pray for him and poor Andrea."

Ray Swift Elk saw the careless movement in the trees ahead. The detachment was already formed up in a skirmish line in anticipation of finishing the small firefight that had sprung up a scant hour previously. He raised his rifle and squeezed off a quick shot. The NVA crumpled under the bullet's impact.

A spattering of fire broke out to the immediate front.

Archie, startled by the shooting, dropped down. He waited a few moments, but no shots came his way. He rose up a bit to scan the area to his direct front. Falconi and Top joined him.

"Anything exciting, Archie?" Falconi asked.

"No, sir. There was some shots, but I ain't seen a thing around here."

"Let's ease forward a bit and see if we can scare up some action," Falconi said.

"You bet, sir," Sergeant Major Top Gordon agreed.

The three Black Eagles, carefully covering each other, walked slowly to the front. They were so alert that their nerves seemed to itch. Not even a leaf dancing in the damp wind escaped their attention.

Finally, Falconi held up his hand. "There's nothing in this sector of the line."

"Damn!" Archie complained. "I almost wish those bastards were strong enough to stand fast and give us a good fight."

"Yeah," Top said, echoing the sentiment. "At least we could wrap this thing up once and for all."

"We will eventually," Falconi said. "Let's not get overanxious."

The same frustrating experience was being shared by the rest of the detachment. But things changed rapidly for Calvin Culpepper and Blue Richards.

A blast of impulsive fire splattered around them, forcing the pair of Black Eagles to dive to the ground.

"Enemy left front!" Blue sounded off when he

spotted the khaki color of NVA uniform.

"Let's go, Blue!" Calvin said.

They leaped up and charged forward, but when they reached the point of contact all they found was some flattened grass where the North Vietnamese had been positioned only moments before.

"Them sonofabitches are giving me a bad case of the ass!" Calvin complained. "They're just slowing us up."

"That's all they can do," Blue surmised. "If you cain't whup a feller, you just punch him on the nose a couple times then hightail it."

He'd no sooner spoken than another volley of incoming fire smacked the trees around them. They dropped to the ground. Wordlessly, they advanced. More shooting exploded in front of them as they moved in for the kill.

"Cover me!" Blue shouted, moving off to the left.

Calvin, without aiming, simply hosed out streams of slugs. Then he followed his partner in the attempt to close with the enemy position. A marked increase in enemy fusillades slowed down their assault to a crawl, then finally forced them to come to a complete halt. The atmosphere was filled with the blasts, smacks, and zings of heavy firing.

"Goddamnit!" Calvin swore. "Now they pinned us down."

But before there was time to worry, Ray Swift Elk's voice sounded from the rear. "Hey, guys! Gunnar and I are here. We'll give you covering fire, then we can move up and take 'em out."

"Go!" Blue shouted.

Gunnar and Swift Elk gave a full minute of

sustained, full-automatic sweeps of the jungle ahead. Then Swift Elk, as the senior, led the small combat team forward. The enemy resisted for a few moments, then broke contact and quickly withdrew.

The jungle settled back into eerie silence.

Dimitri Sogolov, in spite of being a full colonel in the KGB, had never been in combat. He felt a delicious almost boyish thrill as he sat in the North Vietnamese forward observation bunker. The Russian peered through the firing slit out into the rain-drenched jungle ahead. It gave him a real taste of adventure to know that the countryside he peered out into was actually a no-man's-land where combat could erupt at any time.

Truong, beside him, could almost tell what was going through Sogolov's mind. Truong, as a veteran of long campaigning against the French during his earlier army career, felt superior and a bit contemptuous toward the Soviet officer. He pointed out of the bunker. "That," Truong said, "is where the real struggle is. In that contested territory, the comrades sweat and bleed and die." The Vietnamese general almost laughed, knowing that in order to find some accommodating South Vietnamese or American soldier to kill him, Sogolov would have to walk at least three days.

The two stayed at the viewing slit for almost a quarter of an hour. Sogolov's battle reverie was suddenly disturbed by a movement in the jungle.

"What is going on?" he demanded.

Truong, unconcerned because he knew the depth

208

of the defenses in the area, didn't answer for a few moments. Then he saw the NVA troops approaching. "It is the detachment you sent to fetch the prisoner Andrea Thuy."

"Ah, yes," Sogolov said. He went out the back door of the bunker and climbed up the steps to the top. The Russian waited until the prisoner and escort reached him. When he saw Andrea Thuy, he was surprised by her beauty. Even without makeup, wearing a soaked fatigue uniform, her beauty and full figure were apparent. He nodded to her. *"Bon jour, mademoiselle,"* he said. "I am most pleased to meet you."

Andrea said nothing. She looked at the Russian with open contempt. One of the NVA gave her a rough shove, and the column continued on into the outpost. When they reached a communications trench, all went into it. After going down the planked excavation for fifty meters they stopped in front of a bunker with a tarpaulin covering as a door.

The NVA officer motioned to Andrea. *"Di thi di!"* he commanded.

She obeyed and stepped into the room. Sogolov made an immediate appearance. He gestured around the plain chamber. "It is not fancy, but it will keep the rain off your head."

Andrea faced him, but still did not speak.

"You realize you will be going through interrogation," Sogolov said. "You could save yourself a lot of trouble if you were cooperative straight away. Will you tell me about the Black Eagles? Their number? Organization? Weaponry?"

Andrea remained taciturn.

"The game is up for you," Sogolov said. "Why not defect? There wouldn't be much to it, really. After answering all questions, you could make some statements for us. Perhaps some television appearance for the international press would be in order."

Andrea merely gazed at him in a disinterested fashion.

"I'm sure there would be a nice place for you in the new Vietnam," Sogolov said. "You'll find we big brothers in the Soviet Union are most appreciative. Perhaps you could even come to live in Moscow. Wouldn't that be nice?" When she still would not speak, Sogolov sighed. "Very well! You know what is in store for you. I hope you will change your mind, Andrea Thuy. It is horrible to think what intense interrogation would do not only to your physical beauty, but to your psychological health as well."

Andrea watched him leave, knowing that her deliverance was now a remote possibility.

The NVA platoon leader, cold and exhausted, led his few troops into the camp interior. He ignored the curious stares of the Viet Cong guerrillas on the defense perimeter as he went directly to the command post.

His leader, Company Commander Giang, was anxious to hear his report. "How is the tactical situation now?"

"The comrade soldiers are performing this dangerous task to perfection," the platoon leader proudly stated. "I have returned to let you know that the main body of our troops is in position and ready for the final blow against the Black Eagle gangsters."

"Duoc roi!" Giang exclaimed. "You have one more bit of action to pull off. You and your brave men must go out and 'tickle' Falconi one more time. Let him catch up with you, then engage his men. After a few exchanges of fire, break contact and withdraw to the northwest. When he follows you, he will be in the direct center of our pincers formation. They will close around him and end Falconi and the Black Eagles once and forever!"

CHAPTER 18

Archie sat on the ground ignoring the discomfort of his wet ass. He looked up at Lieutenant Colonel Robert Falconi standing in front of him. "I don't mean to show no disrespect, sir. But my answer is: No fucking way!"

Sergeant Major Top Gordon, squatting nearby, took the cigar stub out of his mouth and spat. "The C.O. ain't giving you a choice, Dobbs."

Archie sighed. "If I ain't complaining, how's come I'm being pulled in from the point?"

"Because," Falconi said, "you are worn out."

"No I ain't."

"Yes you are," Falconi said. The concern in his voice was evident. "You've got an emotional involvement here that's driving you beyond good sense."

"Well, sir, I admit I'm worried about Betty Lou. But ain't you worried about Andrea? And how about Malpractice? I can tell you for sure that he's concerned as hell about Jean. She's his wife, for Crissake!"

"That's right," Falconi agreed. "But we haven't been breaking trail for the past few days like you have. I want you to ease back and take a breather. Travel along with Top and me and let somebody else take the point."

"Shit!"

Falconi turned from the scout. "Sergeant Major, send Blue up here."

"Yes, sir."

A couple of minutes later, Blue presented himself to the detachment commander. "You wanted to see me, sir?"

"Right," Falconi answered. "Take the point until relieved."

"Aye, aye, sir." Blue turned to walk out ahead of the unit. He passed Archie still sitting on the ground. "Hey there, you o' Archie you. How's it going?"

"Get stuffed, Blue!"

"Boy! Yo're crankier'n a bee-stung bear that didn't git the honey," Blue said.

Blue moved out ahead of the pack. He walked slowly forward, his eyes darting back and forth. He stopped now and then to listen, but all he heard was the dripping of rainwater cascading down through the thick tree canopy overhead. Blue was at ease in woods or jungle. Brought up in the backwaters of his native Alabama, he was a born and bred hunter. The navy seal training he'd received had only added to those natural skills.

A slight cracking noise sounded ahead.

Blue held up his hand to signal a halt. Dropping down, he moved silently and unseen through the brush. It took him only a short two minutes to spot the NVA positions. After checking out exact locations and numbers, he eased back toward the detachment.

Falconi, waiting for him, took the verbal report. "Weak, strung-out rifle section, huh? Okay. Maybe we can catch and wipe out this bunch." He waved over at Top Gordon. "Form 'em up, Sergeant Major. Here we go again."

Dhang withdrew deeper back into the thick vegetation. Flurries of nervousness nearly made him shake as he realized the close call he had just experienced.

A section of NVA infantry was situated across a portion of the jungle. The young deserter had almost stumbled right on top of them. Now, wet and shivering, but concealed, he settled down to wait out the situation.

His desertion from Nygoyen Li's battalion had been simple, but the circumstance permitting it had been more than a year in the making. Like all conscripts into the Viet Cong, Dhang's service was marked by constant surveillance. He was never allowed to be by himself. Even tending nature's calls over slit trenches in camp latrines was witnessed by a trusted VC.

For more than a year he endured being treated as a potential runaway—which he really was. Dhang, like most Vietnamese peasants, wanted nothing more out of life than to be allowed to plant and harvest his rice between seasons while living with the woman of his choice and fathering a brood of children to run with the others in his home village. But neither communist nor noncommunist would leave his people in peace. It was Dhang's tough luck to be grabbed by the Viet Cong and hauled off to the war. Other young men had been taken to the corrupt army of the South Vietnamese where they at least enjoyed a semblance of physical comfort thanks to the generous Americans who were strong allies of the Republic of South Vietnam.

Dhang always planned to run away, but he was determined to be cagey about it. Too many impatient peasant boys had deserted only to be brought back to face severe physical punishment, which sometimes included facing firing squads. Dhang knew he would have to be in a position that offered him precious time to put a lot of distance between himself and the battalion.

That opportunity had arrived the previous evening when Dhang was on guard duty. Now trusted, he had been assigned to go on roving patrol with another young guerrilla. When they split up to go around the camp supply depot, Dhang headed straight out into the jungle.

He'd been held up momentarily during the route across the North Vietnamese Army sector of the camp, but he finally spotted their guard positions and took a roundabout way past them. Finally, he reached the safety of the deep jungle. He moved through the wet darkness for two full hours before taking his first rest.

As he squatted there to catch his breath, Dhang thought of his home village toward the west. It seemed so wonderful to him about being able to head out that way, knowing he could be there among the familiar thatched huts and rice paddies by dawn.

But instead he turned south.

The nightlong trek had almost come to a halt when he nearly walked into the middle of the unexpected North Vietnamese Army position.

Top Gordon was the first Black Eagle to make contact with the North Vietnamese line. He ducked under a spray of incoming AK47 rounds. Archie Dobbs, behind him, went into action throwing a covering curtain of bullets over the sergeant major. Together, they moved forward, blasting the area ahead of them. When they reached the enemy position, they found only evidence of where the NVA troops had been.

"Those guys still ain't got much fight in 'em," Archie remarked.

"They may be at the end o' their tether," Top remarked. "We might have the ladies and them kids back with us by tomorrow sometime."

"I sure as hell hope so," Archie said.

Back in the rear center portion of the Black Eagle combat formation, Ray Swift Elk and Gunnar Olson were growing impatient. Most of the fighting for them had consisted of running from one part of the battlefield to the other without actually being engaged in the fighting.

"We're a lot like those useless tits on a boar hog," Ray Swift Elk said.

"I don't have to be in the front line to be happy," Gunnar remarked. "But if they want me to lend support fire, that's what I want to do." He took a deep breath and exhaled. "I ain't real happy about running all over the place with this machine gun hanging on me, either. Particularly if I don't do any good with it."

"Okay," Ray Swift Elk said. "Let's go out on our own. As long as we don't stray too far, there shouldn't be any real problem."

"Okay, Lieutenant!" Gunnar replied with enthusiasm. "Let's go."

Swift Elk chose a position between the center and the extreme right flank of their line. He and Gunnar walked side by side, slowly advancing through the sopping bushes in the hopes of making some kind of contact with the enemy.

A burst of fire came at them from their right front.

The two Black Eagles swung the muzzles of their weapons in that direction and blasted away. Between the RPK light machine gun and an AK47 on full automatic, the result was devastating. The volleys blew leaves off trees and bushes, split apart palm fronds, and blew gaping holes into tree trunks.

But the enemy had departed.

Gunnar was about to cut loose with a string of choice Minnesota profanity when two NVA appeared to the far right. He and Swift Elk were just about to fire when shooting broke out on the other side of the enemy. The pair of Red soldiers were blown forward by these shots from their rear.

Ray Swift Elk frowned in puzzlement. "What the hell—"

A Viet Cong guerrilla suddenly appeared by the bodies of the dead North Vietnamese. He held his AK47 above his head to show he wasn't going to fire.

"Please to no shoot me, kind gentlemans," he said in English.

"All right," Swift Elk said. "But keep that weapon up high."

"Yes! Yes!" The Charlie walked forward, smiling and bobbing his head to show his friendly intentions. Finally he reached them. "Hello. My name is Dhang."

Andrea sat on the chair in the bare room of the bunker. The chamber, twelve by twelve feet square, was boarded in on floor, ceiling, and walls. A small electric bulb burned weakly overhead, making the place half dark and menacing.

KGB Colonel Dimitri Sogolov paced slowly around her. After he'd made three circuits, he stopped behind the young woman. "I am disappointed in you, Andrea Thuy."

Andrea kept up her silent game.

"You are a professional," Sogolov said. "And as such, you should comprehend the reality of your situation. You are a prisoner completely cut off from your own people, and wholly at our mercy. We can shoot you, torture you, starve you, or—" He paused. "Show you the respect you deserve."

Andrea listened.

"It is time for you to react in a sensible and prudent manner by cooperating with us. Such conduct on your part will certainly not gain your freedom. I have too much respect to insult your intelligence by trying to convince you of that. But a positive attitude will most certainly gain you an easier confinement. Complete defection will mean only house arrest in Hanoi or any other large city in a socialist nation. I personally guarantee that."

The beautiful prisoner continued to maintain her silence.

"So far we have not made you particularly uncomfortable," Sogolov continued. "You have even been given something to eat and drink. We offered you cigarettes but you do not smoke. You have not even spoken to us."

Andrea stared ahead. Any response on her part would be interpreted as a preliminary sign of giving in. In order to keep the status of the situation as she wanted it, Andrea had to be as nonresponsive as possible.

Sogolov was thoughtful. After a few moments, he positioned himself in front of the beautiful prisoner. "We could remove your clothing as a start. Then follow that up by making you assume uncomfortable positions such as standing on one leg, holding your arms out to your side, or making you sit on a

220

sawhorse." He paused as he resumed his pacing. After another circuit, he stopped. "There is also the treatment of no food or water, no sleep, and perhaps a sharp slap to the face or buttocks now and then. All of that is up to you. I am going away for fifteen minutes. When I return, your conduct will determine the type of captivity you are going to endure."

Without further comment, Sogolov walked through the tarpaulin door. Andrea stared at the canvas sheet, her spirits now sinking despite her emotional battle not to give in to despair.

Deep in her heart, Andrea knew her situation was now hopeless.

Dhang took a drag off the American cigarette. He slowly exhaled and expressed his approval. *"Duoc roi!"*

"We're glad you like the tobacco," Falconi said in fluent Vietnamese. "Will you now continue your revelations for us?"

"Ah, *co, Trung Ta,*" Dhang said politely. "The young ladies are being nicely treated. Except that I am not sure about Andrea. They have taken her to the military outpost south of Ben Quang. I heard the NVA soldiers saying that there is a Russian there to question her."

Falconi cursed. "Goddamnit!" He had been secretly afraid that the Reds would figure out Andrea's true identity. And, sure enough, they'd seen past her cover story. The Russian was most likely a KGB officer sent in especially to conduct the preliminary interrogations before she was taken back for further, deeper examinations in which drugs and brutal physical and emotional torture would be applied.

Dhang was apologetic. *"Toi tec.* I regret giving you such bad news."

"Do not worry, friend," Falconi said. "Now please tell us about the North Vietnamese plans regarding me and my men."

"They plan to draw you into a pincer trap by baiting it with what appear to be weak units. They want to create the impression that you are going against a deteriorating defense to encourage you to press onward," Dhang explained.

"We were falling for that one," Falconi said. "Tell me some more."

Dhang gave the location of the Viet Cong camp where Betty Lou and Jean were being held. Next he revealed where the NVA outpost was where Andrea was confined. He also was able to point out the exact location of the small garrison where the mothers of the sick children had been taken.

Ray Swift Elk, sitting nearby, perked up when he heard that. "It's damned important to get those women back to their families at Nui Dep," he reminded Falconi. "If we don't, the whole concept and operation of using native self-defense militia is going to fall apart."

"Right, Ray," Falconi agreed. "I've got some quick planning to do." The Black Eagle commander sank into several long minutes of deep thinking. Finally he snapped out of it. He nudged Dhang.

"Could you lead the children's mothers back to Nui Dep if we rescued them?"

Dhang nodded. *"Co!* I fought there, remember?"

"Great," Falconi said. "Ray, go get Top and get him over here. We've got a three-part rescue operation to put into effect here."

CHAPTER 19

The Viet Cong sentry walked his post through the empty campground. The North Vietnamese troops had left twelve hours ago to go out into the jungle and set up the big ambush which was to be the final one that would destroy the hated American Black Eagles.

The guard continued pacing back and forth across the abandoned area. It was growing close to dawn, and in the gray light, he dully noted the places where the NVA soldiers had bedded down. The depressions in the soft jungle terrain were now filling rapidly with rainwater. The one thing that the VC did not notice, however, was the man intently watching him from the jungle at the clearing's edge.

Archie Dobbs belly-crawled from under the palm bush. He slithered across the open space toward the guard. When the sentry turned on his circuit, Archie would lie quietly, not moving until the man once more faced the opposite direction.

Finally the Black Eagle scout was in a position

where he could conceal himself in some shrubbery situated along the guard's post. When the VC walked past, Archie silently stood up and moved forward. He locked his arm around the man's throat and, at that exact same instant, drove his knife up under the ribs and into vital organs.

There was only some minor thrashing before the internal hemorrhaging took effect. Archie quietly lowered the body to the ground and emitted a soft whistle.

Top Gordon and Malpractice McCorckel came out of the jungle and crept across the clearing to join Archie. Top looked down at the dead guard. "Nice going."

"Thanks," Archie said. "According to Dhang we go that way." He pointed at a place where a bamboo grove grew along a shallow ravine.

"Let's go," Malpractice hissed impatiently. His wife Jean was now less than a hundred meters from him.

The trio moved toward the bamboo, then slanted off to the east. Within moments they could see the dark outlines of poncho-tents where the Viet Cong were bedded down for the night. At one point, they had to step back into the shadows when a pair of Charlies strolled nonchalantly into the area from another portion of the camp. From the loudness of their voices, the Black Eagles assumed they were not particularly concerned about camp security.

"Prob'ly a coupla officers," Archie whispered with a soft chuckle.

"Yeah," Top agreed. "No self-respecting NCO is going to make that much noise."

Malpractice was irritated. "C'mon! Let's knock off the bullshit and get to the girls."

"Right," Archie said. "Here we go, guys. But be quiet for Chrissake!"

They went through the small tents taking care not to trip over any support lines holding up the structures. Archie led them into a supply depot, seeking cover inside a stack of wooden crates.

"What the fuck are we waiting for?" Malpractice demanded to know.

"Cool it, man," Archie said. "I ain't rushing through this place without taking some time to listen and watch what's going on around me."

"The women are—" Malpractice started to say.

Archie interrupted him. "Don't you think I want to see Betty Lou? I'm in a hurry, too, but I don't want to get caught and have her watch me get blowed away by a firing squad."

"He's right," Top said. "Knock it off, Malpractice."

"Sure, Sergeant Major," Malpractice said, cooling down. He nudged his friend. "Sorry, Archie."

"So buy me a beer when we get back," Archie said. He went to all four sides of the supply position and listened. Finally he returned to the others. "Looks good, guys. We're on our way now."

They skirted across some open ground, moving rapidly until they were into the deep shadows of a tall stand of trees. Once more Archie halted their progress. After a scant half-minute wait, he motioned Top and Malpractice to duck. "Guard!" he whispered.

Archie didn't have time to be fancy. There was no

227

way in hell that the guy wouldn't see him. He simply waited until the VC came close enough, then he went forward in a frontal attack, stabbing the Charlie in the stomach while grasping his face hard to smother any vocal outburst.

Top Gordon, an old campaigner, had swiftly and correctly read the situation. He rushed forward and helped Archie control the sentry until the man died.

"Shit!" Archie said. "Thanks, Top. That could've done it all in for us."

"You're welcome, young man," Top said. "Just tell Malpractice to give that beer he owes you to me."

"I ain't that grateful, Top," Archie said with a wink. He turned and led them on toward their objective. Finally he spotted the lean-to. As he drew closer he could hear the sounds of sleeping children. When he reached the spot, he slipped inside. Betty Lou lay sleeping on her side, a blanket covering her form. Archie bent down to her ear and whispered, "Betty Lou!"

Before she could make an outcry, he covered her mouth.

"It's me," Archie said. "We've come to get you, but you've got to be quiet."

Betty Lou was wide awake. She sat up and threw her arms around Archie, kissing him wetly on the mouth. Malpractice and Jean were going through the same thing on the other side of the tent. Top Gordon stood guard outside, hoping like hell they could get the show on the road before daylight.

Archie spoke fast. "We've got a plan, Betty Lou. There's a nylon twine to link those kids together who can walk. If any need carrying, we can do that, too.

228

What shape are they in?"

"Pretty good now, Archie," Betty Lou said. "There's only two little ones who need to be carried."

"That's fine," Archie said, relieved. "Start waking them up, and keep 'em quiet. We only got a coupla minutes to get outta here. Can we do it?"

"Oh, God, I pray so," Betty Lou said, turning to the tricky task ahead of them.

Falconi scanned the camp through his binoculars. The various cookfires made vision easy. After only five minutes of observation, the Black Eagle commander correctly calculated the strength and disposition of the bivouac's occupants. He also noted the cells constructed of plywood and thick bamboo. Firelight played on the structures, revealing the prisoners confined there—the young mothers of the kidnapped children.

Falconi replaced the field glasses in their carrier. "Okay," he whispered to his companions. "Get into position."

Ray Swift Elk, Paulo Garcia, Blue Richards, and Calvin Culpepper spread out while Falconi pulled back where Gunnar the Gunner Olson waited. The ex-Viet Cong Dhang, carrying his Ak47, also stood close by.

"How do you say 'now' in Norwegian, Gunnar?" Falconi asked.

"'Now'?" Gunnar inquired. He thought a moment. *"Na."*

"Well, then," Falconi said. *"Na,* Gunnar! *Na!"*
Gunnar grinned. *"Ja, jeg forstar!"* He raised the

229

RPK light machine gun, sighting through it at a spot close to the wooden cells. He pulled the trigger, hosing out a fire burst that exploded through the rainy predawn air like a blast of lightning.

Immediately the Black Eagle skirmish line moved forward. Their fire was professional and prearranged. Not a single meter of space along the attack escaped the sweep of the ferocious fusillades of AK47 bullets.

The Viet Cong garrison, a small unit of ineffectives who had been placed there to keep them out of the way, made an attempt to resist the surprise attack. Most of their fire was directed at the middle of the assault, forcing Falconi, Ray Swift Elk, and Gunnar Olson to flop unceremoniously to the ground.

But the Charlies had little time to enjoy this limited success. Blue Richards, coming in from the flank, slipped his selector to full automatic. His fire bursts pounded the hell out of the defenders, causing them to hesitate for a bit.

Paulo Garcia, on the opposite side, had also quickly and correctly reacted to the resistance. With Calvin Culpepper standing behind him to lend his own firing, Paulo raked the Viet Cong with sprays of bullets that overlapped Blue's.

Then the resistance stopped.

The VC broke contact and ran like hell through the misty, rainy dawn. When the Black Eagles reached the far edge of the camp, there wasn't a Red guerrilla left. Only a couple of bodies were sprawled out where they had fallen from the flanking fire.

Falconi pointed to Blue and Paulo. "Cover this

end of the camp 'til we can get out of here." He motioned to Calvin and Dhang. "Let's get the women out of those cages."

The prisoners had huddled in the bottoms of the wooden cells. Now, recognizing the fighting had ended, they got to their feet and crowded the bars. Peering out, they quickly recognized the Black Eagles.

One called out piteously. "Our children! Our children! *Ho o dau?*"

"The boys and girls are safe," Falconi said. "They are with the nurses at a different place. But they will go back to Camp Nui Dep, too. You will meet them on the way and all go back to your men together."

Cries of joy and relief sounded from the stricken women.

"Dhang!" Falconi hollered.

The ex-Viet Cong, still dressed in his black pajama uniform, came forward. He displayed a toothy grin to Falconi. *"Co, Trung Ta?"* he asked.

Falconi put his arm around Dhang's shoulders to show that he was a friend. "This man will be your guide. He is a good friend and can be trusted. Follow him to the spot where your children will meet you with the nurses and three more of my men. Then, together, you will return to Nui Dep. Do you understand?"

The women answered with anxious affirmative shouts.

"Then go!" Falconi shouted.

Dhang motioned to the women, turned south, and started walking. Though tired, their spirits were now buoyed up. They rushed after him, happy and

231

anxious to find their children.

Falconi watched them leave, then turned to his men. "Okay, guys. We've got one more big objective. It's the roughest and most dangerous. Are you ready for it?"

Ray Swift Elk grinned easily. "What's that you always say, sir?"

Falconi smiled grimly. "Nobody said this job was going to be easy!"

Archie Dobbs fidged impatiently. Finally Malpractie came out of the darkness toward him. "Okay," the medical sergeant said. "Ever'body's ready. The kids that need carrying are taken care of, and the others that can walk are formed up in a line."

"Are they all linked together with that nylon twine?" Top, standing nearby, asked.

"Right, Sergeant Major," Malpractice answered. "None of 'em are going to wander off."

Archie turned and led them on a circuitous route from the lean-to. He avoided the main camp, although that route would have been much quicker. The sleeping Viet Cong, inattentive and enjoying a false sense of security because of the North Vietnamese in the vicinity, enjoyed their rest while the rain pattered down on their poncho-tents.

When Archie reached the area where they'd first come in, he paused long enough to look carefully around the immediate area. He could see the dead guard's feet sticking out from under the bush where they'd dragged him. The scout looked back at the anxious people behind him.

232

Betty Lou, holding an infant in her arms, smiled encouragement. Archie winked back at her. He could also see Jean. She held a small child, too, and her husband Malpractice had his arm around her.

Archie's mind thought, *Now or never!* He took a deep breath and stepped out to begin the trek back toward Nui Dep and safety.

CHAPTER 20

Andrea had been alone for a bit more than an hour. After Sogolov left her, she sat quietly in the chair keeping her senses alert in spite of the deep fatigue that drained her energy. She wanted to make sure she was not under surveillance from some hidden viewing point.

She made herself appear casual as she glanced around the room for any unusual appearances in the planked walls of the bunker room where she was imprisoned. There seemed to be none. Windowless and solid, the bulkheads had no mirrors or windows that would give an observer visual access to the chamber. The only obvious place was the canvas tarpaulin over the door, but that seemed unlikely.

Andrea stretched and stood up. Walking slowly, she made a circuit close to the board siding to see if there were any tiny slits that seemed unusual. There were none to detect. She went back to the chair and sat down.

Now she concentrated on instinct, delving deep

into her psyche to see if her innerself perceived the invisible vibrations of another living presence nearby.

There was none.

The beautiful Eurasian woman took a deep breath, held it, then slowly exhaled, making her entire body relax as much as possible in the hard, straight chair. Then her eyes closed, and she slipped into a shallow nap.

The stress and turmoil of the previous weeks took their toll in her dreams. Disjointed, unrelated flashes of mental images filled her troubled sleep. She could see her parents walking through Nui Dep, and she vaguely wondered what they were doing there. Next, Falconi came into the scene and talked with them. Suddenly they were whisked out of sight as if a strong breeze had blown away some paper dolls. Falconi looked at her and waved. Suddenly he also disappeared as Betty Lou and Jean, with all the children, walked across the camp. Then the camp changed into a monsoon-drenched forest. A large male tiger, sopping wet from the rain, strolled into view. He raised his head and opened his mouth, baring his fangs as he emitted a silent roar.

Suddenly Andrea awakened.

A brief exchange of male voices speaking Vietnamese sounded on the other side of the tarpaulin door covering. Andrea, alarmed and wide awake now, listened intently. Then she relaxed as she realized that the only thing happening was the posting of a guard outside the room. That meant there would be no interrogation for a while. But there was no real comfort in that realization.

Andrea knew that it meant the Russian was letting her cool her heels and dwell on the unpleasantness to come.

Gunnar Olson crawled through the sopping wet bushes, careful to keep his machine gun out of the mud. The slimy, cold stuff stuck to his soaked fatigues, making movement more difficult. He ignored the discomfort. His total concentration was on the dangerous job ahead. When he reached the vantage point he sought, the Minnesotan carefully positioned the weapon and laid out a supply of 40-round box magazines beside it.

Gunnar made a double check of his vicinity to make sure he couldn't be spotted. After adjusting some impromptu camouflage in the form of leaves and branches, he settled down to wait.

He checked his watch. It had been synchronized exactly with those of Falconi and Swift Elk, meaning the three men could operate at the exact second if they wanted to—or had to.

Which was the exact case.

Gunnar did not settle into a lethargic mood. He had plenty to do. The first thing was to study the layout ahead of him. All targets of opportunity and potential points of resistance had to be quickly identified. Next he took sight pictures with the machine gun, readjusting the bipod a couple of times to make damned sure he could swing the muzzle to any position he wanted to.

A command bunker was easy to pick out. A small North Vietnamese national flag was mounted in a metal stand at the door. A guard wearing a poncho stood at a position of strict attention. Gunnar wanted to be sure he could hit any NVA officer who came charging out the portal.

The next thing that caught his eye was a small Soviet command car parked on top of the bunker. Gunnar thought that was a hell of a place to leave an automobile, and he made sure he could rake it with a few quick swings of the machine gun's bore.

Another thing that Gunnar could see was a communications trench, complete with planked flooring, that ran from the command bunker back to some well-dug rifle pits. He shook his head on that one. This place as obviously well prepared. In fact, it appeared a bit too fancy to have been a spontaneous combat station quickly established in the heat of battle. The place obviously had not evolved from a tactical situation. Nevertheless, Gunnar stared through the sights of the RPK light machine gun and found he could send fireburst straight down that trench.

A few North Vietnamese troops also milled about. Wearing good grade ponchos and pith helmets, they were too clean-cut and dressed too fancy to be frontline troops. Gunnar shrugged. They would die just as easy as the most dog-eared, worn-out front line rifleman that ever served in any army.

Suddenly a movement caught Gunnar's eye. When he saw the man, he had to look again to make sure he wasn't hallucinating. It was a European, complete with a well-cut khaki uniform that bore blue epaulets. Gunnar put him in his gunsight as well, then grinned to himself.

The afternoon should be a very interesting one.

Falconi checked the drawing in his hands with the layout of the North Vietnamese outpost that stretched out before him. The Viet Cong deserter Dhang had given accurate information as to the layout of the small garrison. And he'd also been correct when he said the NVA never considered the possibility of an attack on the locale. It was undoubtedly a showplace to give VIPs the impression they were at the real fighting front. Actually, it was a good defensive site on one side, but an oblique attack could roll across the entire compound.

The Black Eagle commander folded up the drawing and stuck it in his side trouser pocket. "It's just like Dhang said," he remarked.

Ray Swift Elk, Paulo Garcia, Blue Richards, and Calvin Culpepper were standing farther back in the tree line. All had begun to display a glassy-eyed look as the previous days of trekking through the sodden jungle were taking their toll.

"There isn't much to say," Falconi said. "We all know Andrea is in there someplace. The only way to handle the situation is to hit 'em fast and hit 'em hard. There's not time or room for fancy maneuvering, guys. This is the last showdown and all the money is in the pot."

Ray Swift Elk, his Siouix blood heating up a bit at the prospect of combat, was ready to go. "What's the signal for the attack, sir?" he asked.

"It's all up to Gunnar," Falconi answered. "When things look right to him, he'll start firing. That's when we go in. So let's be fast. Any hesitation or slow-up and our Norwegian machine gunner is going to buy the farm. Any more questions?"

There were none. The group fell silent as they began the vigil of listening to Gunnar the Gunner Olson's 7.62 millimeter chorus.

Andrea relaxed again. The guard outside leaned against the outer wall of the bunker. His job was relatively easy since there was really only one way in or out. In order to dig her way to freedom, Andrea would have to go through thick twelve-by-two planking, two layers of sandbags, then tunnel out through solid ground. There was nothing to do but sit on that damned chair and wait to see what would happen.

Machine-gun fire abruptly broke out in the near vicinity.

This was quickly followed by shots coming from the opposite side of the camp. Andrea stood up and almost cheered. She knew exactly what the score was:

Falconi and the detachment had arrived!

Now the beautiful prisoner knew it was time for absolute coolness and logic in choosing her course of action for the next few minutes. She took a deep breath to calm herself, then tiptoed across the slatted floor to the tarpaulin over the door. She slowly pushed back the covering and looked outside. The guard, upset at the unexpected attack, was peering around looking for guidance or an indication of what was happening.

Andrea slipped outside and took a quick look up and down the trench. Nobody was in sight. A quick couple of steps, then she struck the guard hard on the back of the neck with a short, sharp *shuto* karate chop. The man's head snapped back with a crack as his neck broke.

Andrea had the guy's AK47 in her hand before he hit the ground.

Back up on the other end of the trench, Gunnar was shooting his machine gun with all the concentration and artistry a virtuoso piano player might use on his musical instrument.

A few hardcore NVA riflemen had made an attempt to rush him, but his skillful firing quickly pinned them down. Finally, at the urging of a nearby officer, the enemy soldiers leaped up and launched an impromptu charge. Gunnar started on the left side of the line, stitching the man there with a quick fireburst. He methodically worked the bore over to the left, mowing down the attackers. They collapsed to the mud in a neat row.

Next, Gunnar turned his attention to the Soviet command car parked on top of the bunker. He hosed it from step to stern, finally concentrating some extra shots into the gas tank. The vehicle suddenly exploded and burst into flames as it pitched over on its side.

While Gunnar did his part in the war, Falconi and his companions swept forward in a coordinated line of assault. With AK47's blazing, they crossed the open space between the jungle and the camp, leaping into the garrison's locality over the body of freshly killed NVA.

A couple of individual Reds tried to stop the attackers, but their efforts only earned them early deaths. Individual and group shooting from the Black Eagles crumpled them into pathetic, lonely heaps.

A small fire team of four North Vietnamese came out of a far trench in a flanking attack. They moved swiftly and effectively, their firing gradually building up in crescendo.

Falconi knew they could force him and his men back toward the jungle and break off their assault. If that happened, the battle would be lost then and there.

"Paulo! Ray! Come into the center!"

Immediately figuring out what was going on, the two Black Eagles moved off the flank and turned toward the fresh attack. Their rapid shooting set up a crossfire that caught the NVA riflemen in a sweeping volley.

With that threat out of the way, Falconi continued the assault into the outpost's central area. He and his men ran down short trenches, bounded up over bunker roofs, and crossed open space while spilling more North Vietnamese to the ground.

Andrea wasn't wasting her time, either.

She correctly guessed that the machine gun was being used for both support and to draw pressure off the main attack. Andrea headed toward the incoming AK47 fire. A couple of NVA spotted her and moved toward the communication trench to take her out. But she saw them coming and ducked down.

Pushing herself back against the earthen wall, she waited for them to appear. When they did, she swung out and blasted them into bloody heaps. Coolly using the bodies as a step, she raised her head out of the trench for a quick look.

"Robert! Robert!" she called out when she spotted Falconi. "This way!"

The Black Eagles moved toward her as she covered them with calculated bursts of fire. Within short moments they had leaped down into the trench with them. Falconi had only time for a brief kiss. "That way," he said, pointing toward Gunnar's position.

The six people rushed down the plank walk, leaping over dead North Vietnamese soldiers. When Gunnar spotted them, he briefly lifted his fire until they completed the link-up with his position. Then, wordlessly, the group turned back toward the outpost, hosing it with heavy fire as they headed back deeper into the jungle.

CHAPTER 21

The point man on the Green Beret patrol signaled a halt. The leader, Major Rory Riley, moved forward past the other men until he joined up with him. "What's up, Dewey?"

"Movement to the front," the point man answered. "Kind of careless, but I ain't spotted 'em yet."

"Okay. Let's wait it out for a couple o' minutes," Riley said.

After a few moments they could hear more rustling above the sound of the lightly falling rain. The downpour had dwindled off markedly during the previous twenty-four hours, and the Green Berets were glad of it since it allowed them to hear that much better.

"Who the hell do you think is out there?" the point man asked.

"I don't know, but let's play it cool," Riley told him.

They heard more sound. Then a bush a few

meters in front of them moved a little bit. Both Green Berets raised their M16s, ready to fire.

Archie Dobbs stepped into view, wearing a big grin. "Hi ya," he said. "I thought I'd better let you see me."

"Yeah," Riley agreed. "You came damned close to getting your ass blown away." He tried to look past the Black Eagle. "What's happening?"

"A few folks have come home," Archie said. He turned toward the rear. *"Di ra!"* he shouted.

Suddenly Betty Lou Pemberton and Jean McCorckel, both carrying Vietnamese kids, appeared. They were quickly followed by the rest of the children, their mothers, Malpractice McCorckel, and Top Gordon.

Then Dhang, the ex-Viet Cong, walked out of the brush.

"What the hell is he doing here?" Riley demanded.

"Relax, sir," Archie said. "He's one of us now."

When all had appeared, Riley looked around some more. "You're missing some folks."

"Yes, sir," Malpractice McCorckel said. "They're out to get Andrea. She was compromised and taken off someplace else."

"I hope they get her," Riley said sincerely. He took another look at the women and children. "But at least we'll have some happy family reunions when we have this bunch back at Nui Dep."

"Let's get moving," Sergeant Major Top Gordon growled. "I'm in need of a cold beer and a hot cigar."

Colonel Dimitri Sogolov walked slowly through

the ruins of the outpost. Sprawled bodies of dead North Vietnamese soldiers, raindrops bouncing off their unmoving, bloody forms, lay scattered across the width of the garrison. NVA General Truong Van trailed the Russian, but his eyes weren't on the corpses. Instead, he watched the reaction of the Soviet KGB officer.

"The Black Eagles," Sogolov kept saying to himself over and over. "The Black Eagles. The Black Eagles."

Truong smiled. "A most formidable foe." He could remember the sight of Sogolov crouching in the bunker while the world exploded overhead in small arms fire amidst the scream of dying and wounded men.

Sogolov quickly turned around. "Do I sense a note of admiration in your voice for those capitalist gangsters, Comrade General?"

"You do," Truong replied.

"We have lost an important prisoner, an entire outpost has been practically wiped off the face of the earth, and plans to capture the war criminal Falconi are dashed," Sogolov said.

"That is not all, Comrade Colonel," Truong remarked. He pointed toward the trail that led in from the jungle. A dispirited, dejected column of Viet Cong came slowly into view. They hesitated a moment at the sight of the ruined camp, but quickly recovered and entered the area.

Nygoyen Li spotted Truong. He walked up and saluted. When he spoke, his voice was somber and resigned. "My plan of a monsoon attack failed, Comrade General," he stated flatly. "My battalion is wiped out and all prisoners have escaped."

"The nurses and children, too?" Truong demanded to know.

"Co, Comrade General," Nygoyen Li said. "They were there one evening, but in the morning all disappeared. Two of my sentries were dead from knife attacks." He hesitated, then spoke on. "Another of my camps where the children's mothers were was also massacred. Those captives, too, have gone."

Truong turned to Sogolov and quickly translated the sad report.

The Soviet KGB officer's face blanched and assumed a shocked expression. He turned and walked slowly away, muttering over and over, "The Black Eagles. The Black Eagles."

"There they are!" Archie Dobbs happily shouted. He took his binoculars from his eyes and looked down from the observation tower at the people below.

Betty Lou Pemberton, showered and made up, wore fresh fatigues under her poncho. "Is Andrea with them?"

Archie took another look. "Yeah! I can see her! I can see Falconi and Ray! Hell! I can see everfucking-body!"

"Mind your language, Archie!" Betty Lou snapped up at him. "The children will hear you."

"They can't even understand English!" Archie protested.

"It doesn't matter," Betty Lou insisted. "They'll

pick up the bad words anyway. That's the way kids are."

Falconi, arm in arm with Andrea, walked through the defensive perimeter with Ray, Blue, Paulo, and Calvin following. Gunnar the Gunner, as usual, brought up the rear. He still carried his faithful light machine gun.

Jean and Malpractice came out of the repaired dispensary. Jean cried out in joy and joined Betty Lou in rushing forward to hug Andrea. The other Black Eagles, with Rory Riley and his Green Berets, shook hands with Falconi and the others. The militiamen and their families shouted their own words of welcome to these last returnees from the rescue mission.

Suddenly, in the midst of the celebration, rays of sunlight poured down from the sky. Everyone looked up to see a break in the monsoon clouds.

"It's a sign of peace," Betty Lou said. "I'm sure of it."

"I hope so," Falconi replied. But he knew the struggle in southeast Asia was far from over. He would be taking his Black Eagles back into that deadly jungle again and again. "At least the break in the weather means we can call in some aircraft and have you ladies taken out of here and back to Saigon."

Betty Lou turned to Archie. She said nothing, but looked at him with a silent pleading question in her eyes. He smiled apologetically, his own expression sad. He summed up the answer with one simple statement.

"I am a Black Eagle."

EPILOGUE

The cell door opened and the prisoner was yanked roughly off the wooded bunk. The guard pushed him toward the cell door. *"Di thi di!"* he commanded.

The captive, electric shock burns over his body, was dressed in baggy, striped prison clothing that were too large for him. Barefoot and demoralized, he had once worn the bemedaled uniform befitting his position of colonel in the South Vietnamese Army. But all his former dignity had been beaten and shouted away after months of confinement and torture.

He started to sob to himself as they went down the hall. He knew this would be another session of brutality as they continued to wring him dry of all the intelligence he had on clandestine operations in North Vietnam. He had already told them everything he knew, but the Reds continued to use abusive questioning in order to check and recheck his revelations to them.

But this tme they did not stop at the dreaded interrogation chamber. They went on down to another door. This one opened into a rather plain, but pleasant office.

An NVA major pointed to a neatly folded stack of clothing. "Get dressed!"

The prisoner obeyed, surprised at the quality of the attire. Although it was only a Chinese manufactured denim suit, it felt wonderfully clean and well fitting to him. After dressing, he was ushered by the major out another door and down a hallway. They passed through one more portal and stepped out into an alley where an automobile waited. The captive barely had time to notice it was night before he received another curt instruction.

"Inside!"

The prisoner dully obeyed. After settling in, a young soldier-driver started up the car. They went through the dark streets until they were outside of the city traveling down a rural highway. A half hour later, the car was turned off onto a side road. They finally stopped after going a short distance to a place where another vehicle waited. A high-ranking officer stood by this other conveyance, calmly smoking a cigarette.

"Report to the comrade general!"

The prisoner got out of the car and walked slowly up to the officer. He stopped and looked at the man illuminated by the headlights. The general came close, speaking in low tones. "Do not show surprise or any emotion," he whispered. "I wish to defect

252

from the north. The driver and officer over there know nothing about it."

The prisoner, confused, licked his dry lips. "I don't know what I can do."

"I can get you back to your side through a clandestine E&E net of my own. You can arrange for someone to come and pick me up. Once I am in the south, you can escort me to the right people," the general said. "That is all that I require of you. Do you not wish to rejoin your army and government? Do you not wish to see your wife and family again?"

"Yes," the prisoner said. "But I have betrayed my country under questioning."

"I will tell them you did not break," the general said. "You will be a hero."

The prisoner's hopes rose. "But how do I know I can trust you?"

"Wait." The general left him, walking slowly over to the other car. When he arrived, he engaged the others in conversation, begging a cigarette and match. Suddenly he stepped back, pulling a Russian Tokarev automatic pistol from his holster. He fired twice quickly. Then he turned and beckoned to the prisoner. *"Tien len!"*

The captive obediently went over to the general. He looked down at the bodies in the headlights. Both were truly dead, bits of brains sticking out from their head wounds.

"Now do you believe me?" the general asked.

"Co, Dai Tuong," the prisoner said, nodding.

"Tell them I will be available at the coastal R&R center north of Ha Coi," the general said.

"Ha Coi? That is almost in China!" the prisoner exclaimed.

"It will be dangerous for those who come to fetch me, but I am worth such a risk," the general said.

"Yes. Of course," the prisoner said. "*Xin loi ong*, but whom shall I say is defecting, General?"

The officer smiled. "They will know who I am when you tell them my name is Truong Van."